Fake Plastic World

Fake Plastic World

Zara Lisbon

HENRY HOLT AND COMPANY

NEW YORK

To Jason, Kellen, Cameron, and Scarlett Solano

Henry Holt and Company, *Publishers since 1866*
Henry Holt® is a registered trademark of Macmillan Publishing Group, LLC
120 Broadway, New York, NY 10271 • fiercereads.com

Library of Congress Cataloging-in-Publication Data is available.

ISBN 978-1-250-15631-0

Our books may be purchased in bulk for promotional, educational, or business use. Please contact your local bookseller or the Macmillan Corporate
and Premium Sales Department at (800) 221-7945 ext. 5442 or by email at
MacmillanSpecialMarkets@macmillan.com.

First edition, 2020 / Designed by Liz Dresner

Printed in the United States of America

10 9 8 7 6 5 4 3 2 1

"Either I'm a psychopath in sheep's clothing, or I am you."

—Amanda Knox

CHAPTER 1

JUSTINE CHILDS BROUGHT IN FOR QUESTIONING BY LAPD

I dream I'm back at school. The first day of eleventh grade. Riley and Abbie and Maddie are there wearing tracksuits from Juicy's newest line, and I'm wearing nothing because I've decided I don't need clothes if all I'm doing is going to school. But standing there in the hallway with everyone staring, I can't believe how stupid I am: I voluntarily waived my right to clothing and now I have to go the whole day naked. I try to cover myself with my hands—I have no other options—but my hands start shrinking. They shrink until they're the size of kitten paws. Then they pop off and walk away. I run to the end of the hallway where my locker is and frantically try to work the combination lock using only the bloody nubs where my hands used to be. I try my birth date, 2-2-01, over and over again, but that isn't it. When I try Eva-Kate's instead, 6-13-00, the lock opens with a startling clang. Before I look, I already know what's in my locker. Instead of the spare dress I hoped to find, it's Eva-Kate's body, folded up, her skin purple blue and shriveled, slipping off her shoulders to expose bone.

"Eva-Kate," I breathe. The hallway fades slowly away until it's only her and me in an endless black void.

Her eyes snap open. They're red, blood vessels swollen and breaking apart. When she opens her mouth, it too is red. I understand that she's been biting her lips to a pulp with the tiny white razor blades where her teeth should be.

You did this, she coos, *look at what you did.*

✳ ✳ ✳

On the morning of July nineteenth, I woke in a puddle of my own sweat to the thwacking sound of a fist against my door. The sheets stuck to my skin. I was back in my own bed, Princess Leia at my feet, birds chirping outside my window as if everything were fine, as if I'd never met Eva-Kate Kelly and she'd never been found dead, floating in the canal outside her Venice home. As if I could get up and find her across the bridge, alive and well and day drunk. My head ached. I couldn't believe it had only been the day before when detectives had showed up at my room at the Ace Hotel and told me that she was gone. I missed her.

"Justine?" My mom's voice was strained on the other side of my door. "Justine, are you up?"

I sank back into the sweaty sheets as the memory of yesterday slowly pieced itself together in my addled brain.

✳ ✳ ✳

Detectives Trevor Sato and John Rayner said I wasn't required by law to come to the station, but if I wanted to help them find out what had happened to my friend, it was in everyone's best interest that I go with them. I did want to find out and I did want to help. What I didn't want was to wallow alone in this dread, hot and slippery and deep purple red like the inside of a throat swallowing me whole. So I went. Teeth chattering, head spinning, free-falling.

The room they pulled me into was sterile and cold. I held Princess Leia close to keep warm.

The walls were a diluted green color, but everything else—the table, the chairs, the floors, the ceiling—was made up of different textured metals, some brushed, some polished, some corrugated, all of it more than a little bit neglected. On a steel rod suspended from the ceiling hung a single light bulb housed within a steel cone, like something you'd put on a dog after surgery.

And the air-conditioning was cranked up to unreasonable heights. I hadn't thought to put a bra on before being whisked into the cop car and so my nipples pressed like pushpins against my cotton T-shirt. From my chair I looked up at Detective Sato to see if he noticed. He didn't. Or he was good at pretending not to notice. Or he noticed but didn't care.

He sat across from me with his arms crossed and his elbows resting on the table. He cleared his throat, looked at the clock above my head, looked at his notepad, looked at me. With his strong jaw and dimpled chin, he reminded me of Gaston from *Beauty and the Beast.* Those muscles and that palpable arrogance. I tried to guess at what he was thinking, but his eyes were steel doors slammed shut, blocking me out. Not knowing made me sweat a little, even trapped in the frigid AC as I was. The blissfully numbed-out summer had made me forget how uneasy I became when I couldn't get a read on somebody. When I couldn't tell what they thought of me. I really hated that.

"So . . . ," I built up the courage to ask, "are you going to, uh, ask me questions or—"

"Not quite yet," he said before I was finished. "Soon."

The door swung open and in came Detective Rayner. Tall, balding with some white hair slicked back, narrow-rimmed glasses resting in front of blue eyes with a grandfatherly glint. He held steaming coffee in a Styrofoam cup. The cup was tiny, almost in a funny way, and made me think of the *Titanic* exhibit my parents took me to when I was just four or five. To demonstrate the unimaginable pressure that exists four hundred miles below sea level, they displayed a regular-sized Styrofoam cup—six inches tall or so—and next to it the same cup after having spent time at the bottom of the ocean. That second cup was hardly bigger than a thimble. This terrified me. Something about the covert power of water and what it could do to a thing—to *me*—if it had the chance, really knew how to keep me up at night. Seeing the cup in Rayner's wrinkled hand brought the chill back.

I imagined Eva-Kate floating in that dirty canal water, drowned. I imagined her wading out up to her ankles, probably drunk. Maybe she tripped. Maybe somebody pushed her. I tried hard not to imagine that final moment, the one where she knew it was over.

"Would you like something to drink, Justine?" Rayner asked. "Water? Sprite?"

"Could I . . ." I heard my own voice, thin and webby. "Could I have some coffee? Please. If possible." I'd slept plenty, but that didn't keep me from feeling exhausted. For as long as I could remember, sleep had never done much for me at all. When people spoke of being refreshed after an amazing night's sleep, it sounded at best like a foreign language, at worst like a horrible lie. I carry with me a long list of envies, but there's nobody

I envy more than those who can wake up feeling ready for the day.

"Coffee, huh?" He stood behind Sato. "Aren't you a little too young for coffee?"

"No . . . I don't think so. I'm sixteen."

"Coffee stunts your growth, you know that?"

"In Europe they let their kids drink coffee," I offered. Sato laughed.

"Sure," he said. "If they do it in Europe, *surely* it can't be that bad."

Rayner walked back to the door and pulled it open a crack. "Luanne?" he called out. "Would you be a dear and get us a cup of coffee?"

"Cream or sugar?" a voice called back, husky but sweet. Rayner looked to me for the answer.

"Black, please."

"Neither," he told her. "Thanks, Luanne." He shut the door and took a seat next to Sato.

"Black coffee?" asked Sato. "You're pretty tough."

"Sorry?"

"To take coffee without cream or sugar. That's bitter stuff. Strong. Most grown men don't even drink it that way."

"I never get the proportions right, I always ruin it. It's easier to just leave it as it is."

"Is that right?"

"You know, in Europe, coffee isn't the only thing

they start drinking young," said Rayner. "Any chance you're . . . *European* in that way too?"

"I don't know what you mean," I said, though I did know. *Why does he want to know if I drink? What does that have to do with Eva-Kate?* I told myself he was trying to figure out if *she* was a drinker, if that could be part of what happened to her.

"Alcohol, Justine," he said. "Can I call you Justine?"

"That's my name," I said. I couldn't think of what else he'd call me.

"Do you like to drink, Justine?"

I'd seen enough TV to know I didn't have to answer that. I shrugged and crossed my arms. When they started asking me questions about Eva-Kate's death, questions I could help with, that's when I'd start talking.

"You're not ready to tell us." Sato nodded. "That's fine. We—" The woman I assumed was Luanne came in then with my coffee. She had curly red hair held in a half updo with a tortoiseshell clip. Pale lipstick, clear-rimmed glasses. She set the cup down before me and I picked it up with a shaky hand. I figured I must be hungry, though I didn't feel it. I wanted to thank her but it suddenly felt like the hardest thing to do.

"Nancy Childs is here," she told the detectives.

I put the cup down. "My *mom*?" I choked. "But she's . . . she's not even . . . she's been traveling. What about my dad?"

"Maybe she's *been* traveling, but she's here in LA now."

Already? I winced, remembering the voice mail.

Hi, Eva-Kate, this is Dr. Childs. I'm calling to let you know I'll be back in Los Angeles next week, and will be available to resume our evening sessions on Tuesday. Looking forward to hearing from you, bye for now.

I tried to swallow down the lump in my throat, but either it was too big or my throat was too tight. My whole life I'd been the victim of a particular cycle. Something would make me nervous, and being nervous would make my throat tighten. Then feeling my throat closing would send a much stronger alarm signal to my brain, telling it something was wrong, which would effectively elevate my nerves to a level of acute anxiety. The more anxious I became, the tighter my throat got. At Bellflower I learned techniques to stop the wave of panic before it became tidal. Breathing techniques, counting techniques, visualizing techniques. My go-to visualization was of Taylor Swift and her cats, Meredith and Olivia, huddled on the window nook in her West Village apartment. I closed my eyes and went there now. I counted to ten.

"Send her in," said Rayner. "Thanks, Luanne."

I took a big gulp of coffee and held it in the back of my mouth, appreciating the piping hot, hazelnut smolder.

My mother stormed into the room, already furious.

She was tanner than when I saw her last, and less wrinkled, if that was possible. She'd gained some weight and was wearing a breezy lilac tunic. Her hair had grown out a bit and she'd gotten it straightened. She looked like a different person. I saw her see me and think the same thing, which satisfied me, if only a little.

"Don't say anything, Justine," she said as she rushed to me and put both hands on my shoulders. "You don't have to say anything to them."

"I know that," I said, shaking her off. "But I want to help." I wondered if she knew what had happened or why we were here. How much had they told her?

"Mrs. Childs, we just want to figure out how Eva-Kate died. We believe your daughter—"

"Eva-Kate?" She froze, clutching the cameo pendant that hung from her neck. "*Eva-Kate Kelly?*"

For a second I thought she'd burst into tears. *She didn't know.* I felt her cross over, joining me in the realm of shock.

Sato and Rayner shared a glance.

"That's correct, Mrs. Childs," said Rayner. "I apologize; I thought you were informed on the phone."

"Dr. Childs," she said. "Please."

"Of course."

"I don't understand." She started pacing unevenly, cracking her knuckles. "How can my daughter help you?"

"Justine and Miss Kelly had become pretty close over the summer."

"Close? How would . . . ?" She looked to me. "Justine?"

"Eva-Kate moved into the house across the canal." I watched her face stiffen as she took this in. "We met a few weeks ago."

She paused for several moments. The color faded from her face.

"Oh God." She shook her head, calculating the significance. "The house *across from our house*? Jesus." I knew what she was realizing, though of course Rayner and Sato did not. She caught their quizzical glances and composed herself.

"Justine," Rayner said, "can you tell us where you were two nights ago?"

"I was . . . first I was at home. Then I left and went to the Ace Hotel, which is where I was when—wait." I realized something. "How did you know to find me there?"

Rayner jotted this down on a notepad inside the leather folder he'd been resting his heavy hand on like a Bible.

"Instagram, sweetheart," said Sato. "Hint: Next time you're in hiding, don't post to social media."

"But I didn't . . . I only posted a picture of Princess Leia, that doesn't . . ."

"We traced the location of the post. It was geo-tagged."

"*What?* Are you even allowed to—"

"The Ace Hotel?" My mom's brow furrowed. "Why would you go—you know what, never mind." She turned from me to the detectives and said, "She doesn't have to answer that."

"Dr. Childs," Sato said with both palms placed flat against the table, pressing down his own mushrooming frustration. "Your daughter isn't under arrest, we're simply asking for her help. As we said, Justine had become very close with Eva-Kate, and we're hoping she can give us some insight into who might have done this to her."

"*Done this to her?*" I repeated. "You think someone *did* this? You don't think it was an . . ."

"An accident?" Sato finished my sentence, shaking his head. "Definitely not." He put his hand out to Rayner, who produced a photograph from the folder and slid it facedown to him. Sato flipped it faceup and slid it across the table to me.

In high definition, crystal clear, was the athame Eva-Kate had showed me. The five-inch dagger, handle painted white with little blue cornflowers and a decorative green tulle bow. It would have looked like a toy, a knife for a doll, if it weren't for all the blood. Eva-Kate's blood. My stomach twisted.

"*What is that?*" my mom asked, chin twitching. "Justine, you do *not* need to be here."

"*Mom*," I said, biting back my own tears, "stop."

"You know what this is, don't you?" Sato asked me.

"Yeah, um." I wiped my eyes with the backs of my thumbs. "It's an athame. It was Eva-Kate's."

"Do you know what she used it for?"

I paused. I saw her sitting drunk on the bedroom floor that night wanting to make Rob fall back in love. I couldn't say *It's used to cast spells*, or anyway I couldn't say it with a straight face.

"No," I told them. Then, eager to get them as close to the truth as I was capable of, I added, "But I mean, I know it's like a tool that can be used in certain . . . rituals."

"I see," said Rayner. "Did *you* ever use this tool for such . . . *rituals*?"

"Me? No. I wouldn't know . . . I mean, I don't necessarily believe in the, uh . . ."

"You don't believe in witchcraft," Sato cut in. "Is that what you're trying to say? Eva-Kate was fooling around with this knife thingy trying to cast crazy spells and all that jazz, but the dark arts aren't really your bag?"

"Well, no, but I don't know if she was—I mean, I don't know if she took that stuff seriously or if she was just, you know . . . playing?"

Sato and Rayner shared another glance. My mother tapped her middle three fingers against her forearm faster and faster until they almost hummed. Sato gave Rayner a nod, a sort of go-ahead.

"Justine, I know you've been through a lot," he said, treading lightly along the line between sensitive and scrutinizing. "Losing such a close friend is immeasurably traumatic, and it's possible you don't remember all the details clearly. So, I'll ask you again to be sure: In the time that you knew Eva-Kate Kelly, did you ever use the athame?"

"No, I already said no." I crossed my arms. "I never would . . . why would I? You think *I* tried to cast some kind of *spell*?"

"Excuse me." My mother knit her eyebrows so close together they almost met at the bridge of her nose, turning her forehead into a bundle of well-moisturized grooves. "Detective Rayner, does my daughter need a lawyer?"

"No, Dr. Childs, we don't think—let me rephrase the question." Rayner ignored my mom, rubbing his temples. "Have you ever *held* this athame? The one in this picture?"

"No! It's not mine. Eva-Kate showed it to me once, but *that's it*."

"And you're sure about that?"

"Of course I'm sure."

"They're testing it for fingerprints as we speak," Sato cut in. "Now would be the time to tell us if yours are on it."

It's not possible. The words were on the tip of my tongue, locked and loaded. But then I saw myself— maybe a week ago, maybe two—sitting on the floor of Eva-Kate's room. I heard her voice: *Here, hold it. Feels really empowering.*

I saw her take my hands and wrap them around the handle. I felt the kid gloves she wore stroking the backs of my hands and then the nape of my neck. I smelled the liquor on her breath and shivered.

"Justine?" Rayner brought me back to the room.

"I'm sorry, yes. Actually, I . . . I did touch the athame. Once."

"But you just said you didn't."

"I had forgotten," I explained. "That night was a blur."

"That night? The night Eva-Kate was killed?"

"Oh, I can't handle this." My mom pulled a chair out from beneath the table and let herself collapse into it.

"No! Not that night. This was a different night. About a week or so ago."

"So then the night Eva-Kate died . . . you *didn't* hold the athame?"

"Definitely not."

"Hm, well"—Sato smirked—"that's not what Josie told us."

"*Josie?*" I almost laughed; it was too absurd. "What did Josie say?"

I went over those final moments with Eva-Kate in my mind, but couldn't spot Josie. We'd gotten back to her place, I'd heard my mom's voice on the answering machine, I'd gone home, sneaking around the back so nobody would see me. Now that last part seemed a huge mistake. I hadn't wanted to be seen, but now all I needed in the world was a witness.

"Says she saw you take the knife from a ledge in Eva-Kate's hallway soon after you got home from, uh . . ." He glanced back at his notes. "San Luis Obispo."

"But I didn't. She lied to you."

"Why would somebody lie about that?"

"I don't know!"

"Do you want to tell us what you *do* know about what happened that night?"

"Eva-Kate and I got home, back to her place. Then I left to feed Princess Leia. Then I checked into the Ace Hotel."

"Now, why would you do that? Seems rather . . . spontaneous, no? You had Eva-Kate's home *and* your own to choose from, right? Or are you always checking into hotels in the middle of the night?"

"I was at the Ace," I repeated in lieu of an answer. "I checked in around four or five in the morning. And before that I was at home. So whatever happened to Eva-Kate"—I could feel my blood sugar plummeting, a hot, urgent quaking in my veins and belly—"I had nothing to do with it. And I'd like to go home now."

Rayner sighed. "We'll have to corroborate that with the Ace," he said, gesturing to the door with his pen. "Until then, you're free to go."

CHAPTER 2

JUSTINE CHILDS CONFRONTS MOTHER

I stayed numb and silent in the back seat of my mother's 2013 forest-green Land Rover, but as soon as we got home I started to sob. I clutched Princess Leia to my chest and let her fur soak up my tears. Eva-Kate was dead and I couldn't help but feel guilty. If I hadn't left that night, maybe she'd still be alive. Or something like that. I had a way of being able to make anything my fault.

"Justine, sweetheart." My mother went to hug me, a strain of pity in her voice, a collection of silver bracelets jangling on her wrist. "There's not much in this life more painful than losing a friend. It doesn't matter if you only knew them for a short time. I don't know what to say."

I pulled away. "I know you knew her," I said. "I know

everything." Of course, I didn't know everything. I only knew what I'd read in the papers from my mother's office. I feared there was more.

"What are you talking about?"

"I'm talking about Eva-Kate. I know she was your patient."

She faltered, made an open oval shape with her mouth, then let it fall shut. Then opened it again. Then closed it and put one finger to her sealed lips. Finally, she spoke.

"I can't confirm or deny that, Justine; you know about doctor-patient confidentiality."

"I don't need you to confirm or deny it," I shot back. "I'm telling you that I know. I found your files on her. I read through them. You made the cabinet combination her *birthday*? I don't even know where to begin on how fucked up this is."

I didn't know I'd say it until I said it.

"*Excuse me?*" Her eyes bulged. "You did *what*?"

"I had to." I felt odd and off balance explaining myself as I accused her. "I was afraid."

"Afraid of Eva-Kate?" She sat down next to me, suddenly sweet and shielding. She was like that. She could be crazed with outrage one minute—no, one *second*—then remorseful and atoning the next.

"Yes, of Eva-Kate. She was unwell and you knew it, but you—"

"What happened, angel? Will you tell me?"

I looked down at her feet. They were in silver Birkenstocks, toenails painted pale metallic blue. I couldn't remember the last time I'd seen her in vacation mode.

"*What happened?* Um, let's see . . . Eva-Kate moved in and we became friends. I thought it was weird a girl like her would want to be friends with a girl like me, but I figured stranger things have happened. Then one night, I guess it was two nights ago, I heard you leave her a *voice mail* about scheduling a *session*. I confronted her about it, asked her why she never told me you were her therapist, and she brushed it off like it was no big deal. She said you knew she was buying that house and you were okay with it, which I knew couldn't be true."

She smiled lamely.

"Your instincts were on point," she said. "Good for you."

"So I left," I went on. "I couldn't be around her, it was all too surreal. I came back here looking for more information. And I found it. She was obsessed with me all along and you knew that."

"But I didn't have any reason to believe she would do something as drastic as this, for God's sake."

"But you let her into our house on a regular basis. For years."

"I was the girl's doctor, Justine. It was my job to help her."

"At the expense of my safety?"

"Now you're being a little dramatic." She scratched at a patch of skin beneath her right eye. "She never said anything about wanting to hurt you or anybody else. She was never anything other than curious. Intensely curious, but still, that's what I believed it was. A harmless fixation. That was my professional opinion. Was I wrong? She didn't hurt you, did she?"

I thought about my answer. She had, only not in the way my mom meant.

"No," I said. "She just . . . lied."

"Okay then," she sighed and stood up, wiping a tear off her cheek. "This is all an awful ordeal, but I'm not at liberty to discuss Eva-Kate any further. I'm going to make some tea. Chamomile?"

"Wait," I said. "Tea? You can't just move on like that. You were her therapist, you knew her better than anybody. Don't you want to figure out who did this to her?"

"I *didn't* know her better than anybody else." She turned back, her face tight and controlled, a twitch above her eyebrow. "And it's *not* our job to solve this, Justine. If the police need my help, they'll ask for it. And if they do, I'll tell them everything I know."

"Will you tell them the 'harmless' fixation went both

ways? Will you tell them the passcode to your file cabinet is her birth date?"

She stared, unblinking. She looked to the door, as if for a way out, then sat back down next to me. Her hands quivered as she spoke.

"It's not what you think," she said. "I set that combination years ago when Eva-Kate was still a kid. Her mom had forgotten her birthday and she was hysterical, okay? I was just trying to cheer her up."

Her mom had forgotten her birthday? I wanted to believe my mother, but I didn't know if I should. It didn't quite feel right; if Debbie had forgotten Eva-Kate's birthday, she would have had to forget Liza's too. What kind of stage mom forgets her twin daughters' birthday?

"Fine," I sighed, wanting the conversation to be over, "whatever you say. I just want to be alone."

"Hey, wait," she said. "Why weren't you at Aunt Jillian's? You *were* staying at Aunt Jillian's, *weren't* you?"

"It's not her fault," I said. "I was determined."

"Dammit, Justine. What has gotten into you? If I'd known you'd choose this summer to become so . . . so *reckless*, I wouldn't have left."

"Yeah, well," I said, turning to go, "clearly you shouldn't have."

CHAPTER 3

FRENEMIES? JOSIE BISHOP AND JUSTINE CHILDS SEEN QUARRELING AT VENICE, CALIFORNIA, CRIME SCENE

*T*he sky had darkened, bringing a slight chill to the air, one of those odd July nights sounding a false alarm of summer's end. I grabbed a hoodie and went outside.

From the porch swing I could see the excitement fading across the canal. After the police and their yellow tape had come, the reporters showed up with their microphones and their insensitively excellent hair. The big networks—NBC, CNN, CBS, FOX—had set up trucks on her front lawn, their fat antennae reaching into the sky like overgrown bean stalks. Next the paparazzi had showed up, swarming in clusters, lighting the canal with their flashbulbs going off in vain. Eva-Kate's body was long gone. There was nothing to photograph but the empty crime scene. Having gotten their shots, they were mostly all packed up and gone, at least for today.

Who could have done this?

My stupid heart ached. It gnawed at itself, pulled and clawed at itself. All at once I missed her and feared her. I wanted her here with me, and I wanted to have never met her. I felt she could come for me at any minute, and I had to remember over and over again that somebody had already come for her.

She was gone. But was I safe? Not knowing what she'd wanted from me made it worse, not knowing what her feelings really were. Over and over I came back to the first night on her roof when she'd fastened that gemstone necklace around my neck and let her lips rest against mine for just a second, like an accident waiting to happen. I wanted that back. I needed to kiss her again, even just one more time, to prove it had all been real.

I wanted to believe that Eva-Kate loved me, that she thought of me as special. When a person is gone, how can you know for sure that what you had with them was real? I listened to "All Too Well" by Taylor Swift on repeat, finding comfort in her attempt to make sense of the time she spent romantically entangled with Jake Gyllenhaal.

The song tells the story of a romance that is quaint yet epic, charm-filled and "rare," yet doomed by the man's immaturity and unwillingness to grow up. The way she repeats this over and over ends up sounding as though she's trying to convince herself of these facts, which exposes her raw insecurity, her lack of faith in the experience as it happened. So, my question, even though it is for sure none of my business, is: Was it rare or is that just what Taylor needed to believe?

Because we don't know the answer, the song is disorienting. In some moments we are left wondering what is real and what is Taylor's imagination. Is this how it really went down? Or is it the sparkling, swiftified version of what happened?

I hated myself. How could I obsess over a Taylor Swift song when Eva-Kate had been stabbed to death? I should have been wondering who could have done this; I should have been thinking about her killer.

Her killer. It sounded so intimate, like a thing that belonged to her. Her name, her birthday, her killer. The person who killed her would be hers forever, same as the person who gave her life. I needed a cigarette, or better yet a whiskey on ice, to slow my racing thoughts.

Just then I saw Josie across the canal, walking up to Eva-Kate's house with a giant Louis Vuitton suitcase in hand. She stood out from the growing darkness in red striped Gucci jogging pants and tortoiseshell sunglasses so big it looked like she had two baby turtles for eyes. I shot up and power walked across the bridge. The asphalt scraped my bare soles but I didn't mind.

Eva-Kate's front door was barred by sticky yellow police tape, but Josie didn't let that deter her. She slung her bag over her shoulder and walked around to the side of the house, looking for a way in.

"Hey!" I called out, catching up with her in the backyard. "What are you doing?"

Josie jumped, startled, then saw it was me and sighed so deeply it was almost a groan, both relieved and irritated. Beneath the sunglasses her cheeks were red and mottled and wet. Her lips looked stung and raw.

"Hey," I said again, "I wouldn't go in there. It's a crime scene, you're not allowed to—"

"I don't give a fuck what you would do," she snarled, her voice gravelly and hoarse. "I have a lot of stuff in there that I need, so, if you'll excuse me."

She turned back around and kept walking.

"No." I grabbed her wrist. "We have to talk. I know you spoke to the police."

"So?" She spun to face me, little more than two inches of space between us. Her breath smelled like liquor and I was jealous.

"So why the hell would you tell them you saw me take the athame from the hallway?"

"Fuck, Justine, do we have to have this conversation right now? I just want to get my things and leave before someone interrogates me again about the death of my lifelong best friend, if you don't mind."

"I do mind! Josie, you threw me under the bus. If it weren't for the fact that I was at the Ace that night, they'd think it was me who did this."

"You were at the Ace?" Her face slackened. The sour bite in her voice dissolved into milky bewilderment. "Why? When did you go there?"

"Well, first I went to my mom's around ten and stayed there till four-ish. Then I went to the Ace. So, I guess I got there sometime around four thirty. I'm not totally sure," I said. "But I know I wasn't here."

"I could have sworn you were . . ."

"I wasn't. But *you* were. Is that why you told them you saw me take the knife? As a way to get the attention off yourself?"

"Excuse me?"

"Whoever points the finger," I said as if reciting a universally accepted truism, "is almost always responsible."

"Yeah right," she said, hoisting the emblem-dappled bag up so that it rested on her jutting hip bone. "That's not a thing. Everyone knows it's the boyfriend that's almost always responsible. Ex-boyfriend, in this case."

"You think this could be Rob? Then why would you tell them it was me?"

"I didn't tell them it was you. I told them I saw you take the knife."

"Why?"

"Because I did."

"No you didn't! I don't know what you thought you saw, but—"

SNAP SNAP . . . SNAP SNAP SNAP!

The cameras snuck up behind us, shooting painful bursts of silvery-yellow light into the air, breaking my vision up into haloed white spots.

Josie, who killed Eva-Kate? FLASH What were you two just fighting about? FLASH Justine, how are you holding up? FLASH Where were you the night she died? FLASH Who was the last to see her alive? FLASH FLASH FLASH!

They didn't want answers, just visual reactions, expressions to steal right off our faces. I hid mine.

"LEAVE US ALONE!" Josie shrieked at them. "Go back to your moms' basements, you fat fucks!"

With their attention on her, I slipped away, pulling the hoodie up over my head and the top half of my face so that only my mouth showed. I had to keep my eyes angled down so I could see where I was going. My heart pounded along with my feet as they smacked the pavement. They looked so starkly white against the asphalt, white and dew-wet and flecked with dirt. I saw their exposed vulnerability, felt it deep in my gut, and I was ashamed.

✖ ✖ ✖

Again I dreamed feverishly and woke to the sound of a fist against my door.

"Justine?" My mom's voice was strained on the other side of the wood. "Justine, are you up?"

"I am now," I grumbled. There were no locks on my door—my mom had never allowed them—and so she pushed it open and let herself in. She held her laptop, screen open, so that it made an L shape in the crook of her elbow. She fluttered to my bed, cheeks flushed, mouth curled into a sour crescent.

"You haven't seen this yet," she said, thrusting the computer at me. "It's from this morning. I don't know what you were thinking, Justine, I really don't."

I sat up so I could see. The article was from the *Daily Mail*, if you could call it an article at all. A grainy gallery of photographs beneath the headline: *Frenemies? Josie Bishop and Justine Childs Seen Quarreling at Venice, California, Crime Scene.*

I groaned, slammed the screen down against the keyboard. I'd been expecting this, but seeing the words in print, seeing myself from an intruder's perspective, made me sick.

"I don't know what you were thinking," my mom said again. "What were you thinking?"

"I wasn't," I said, falling back onto my pillow and putting one hand over my eyes. It was too bright. *Fuck the sun*, I thought. *Fuck the* Daily Mail.

"Well, that much is clear," she huffed. "Justine, this is serious. Do you have any idea what a big deal traipsing into a crime scene like that is? Any idea how bad it makes you look?"

"I just want to find out who could have done this to her," I said. "Don't you?"

"I want to let the detectives do their jobs," she said. "I *do not* want *my daughter* getting any more tangled up in this . . . this *tragedy* than she already is. Do you understand me? I mean, *my God*, I guess I can't take my eyes off you for one second, can I? I've been so naive."

"So have I," I said, thinking again of combination locks.

"From now on you're not leaving this house without my permission. I'm your mother." She said it as if trying to convince herself. "It's my job to look out for you."

"Fine." I pulled the blankets up to my chin, needing to feel the soft comfort of weight on my body. "But I'm going to the funeral tomorrow."

"Ha!" She let out a cynically amused quacking sound. "That's rich, Justine."

"It's rich to go to my best friend's funeral?" I sat back up for effect.

"She wasn't your best friend, sweetheart, you knew her for a week."

"It was more than a week," I said through gritted teeth. "And I'm going."

"And expose yourself to the paparazzi again? The reporters? Not to mention the legions of parasitic teens with their *camera phones*. I know what they can do, Justine; they can ruin you. I've seen it. Too many times."

"If I don't go . . . ," I said, knowing how I'd convince her. "If I don't go, I'll look guilty. All her other friends will be there. Tell me how *you* think it will look if I'm not."

She bit down on the inside of her cheek and looked diagonally away from me, down to the floor, where Princess Leia was gnawing fiercely at her own paw.

"Yes, fine, you're right," she conceded finally. "But you need to dye your hair back first. This blue is . . . disturbing."

I rolled my eyes. Of course she thought it was disturbing. Anything I did without her permission was disturbing.

"I'll go pick up the dye," I said.

"Nice try," she acknowledged, standing up and plucking her computer off my wilderness of blankets. "Anything else you need at Walgreens?"

If you see my old life, I thought, *the one where you weren't here and Eva-Kate was still alive.*

"No, thank you."

"If you think of anything, text me."

"I don't have a phone," I told her. "It broke."

"What happened to it?"

"It broke," I said again, remembering how I'd smashed it to pieces the night Eva-Kate died.

"Well, you'll need a phone," she said uneasily. "You can have my old one. I'll stop by Verizon on my way home to have them program it."

I didn't know how to tell her I could afford my own phone, nor did I want to. Having my own money gave me power, and keeping it a secret multiplied the power exponentially. If I let her know about it, I'd be giving some of that power away. They say you're only as sick as your secrets, but sometimes your secrets keep you safe.

When I was sure she was gone, I padded out into the living room. I took an unopened bottle of Seagram's and hauled it back to bed with me. I looked around for a glass but gave up easily and drank from the open neck.

Oh, thank God, I thought, swallowing. I would have said the words out loud but chose to keep my mouth shut to savor the burn of whiskey pouring down my throat. It was my first drink since they'd dragged me from the Ace, since learning Eva-Kate was gone, and it felt heaven-sent. I drank until I felt a sweet and merciful relief from the grip Eva-Kate had on me. She held me tighter than ever now that she was dead.

From my window I could see the scene outside her house with a few people starting to gather again. Maybe my mom was right that I shouldn't have gone over there, but I was glad I had. *It's almost always the boyfriend*, Josie had said, *or in this case, the ex-boyfriend.*

She was right, of course, and I should have thought of it on my own. Rob Donovan. Eva-Kate had been black-mailing him, that was as good of a motive as there'd ever be. I knew where he lived. Too bad I'd found myself under house arrest. And even if I were free to go, was I ready to see more of my face speckled across digital tabloid pages? It's what I used to dream about, what I'd always wanted, but not like this. So I'd hide from them, keep my head low. I prayed Rob was stupid enough to be at the funeral.

CHAPTER 4

JUSTINE CHILDS ATTENDS EVA-KATE KELLY FUNERAL . . . WEARING BLUE

The morning of the funeral I woke up early with a bad feeling. I wanted her back, and I couldn't have her. Knowing she would soon be six feet under made the whole thing official, irreversible. There was nothing to be done and I panicked, just like I panic whenever I think about how there's nothing to be done about the inevitability of my own death.

The doctors and counselors at Bellflower would smile and say things like, *There's nothing you can do about it, so there's no point in panicking!* I don't know what planet these people were living on, but on my planet, helplessness is in no way a good argument for a laid-back mentality. They'd say it as if it were good news, as if I could finally choose to relax, as if I had that choice.

My panic is inhuman, with a mind and a plan of its own, and when it rolls in, it constricts my throat, it constricts my chest, it constricts my veins so the blood can't flow and my vision so that all I can see is a tunnel of white light sucking me away from myself. I popped half a Xanax and swallowed it with a swig of Seagram's. According to the pink Kit-Cat Klock, it was barely six in the morning.

In the bathroom I found a box of Garnier Nutrisse hair dye waiting for me on the sink counter. The box read: *Nourishing Color Creme, #413 Bronze Sugar.* Lazy and impatient, I put on the recommended rubber gloves and streaked the chemical compounds through my hair. The smell of hydrogen peroxide and ammonia made my eyes water. It stung the inside of my nostrils every time I inhaled. But I didn't hate it. I almost liked it, like if I inhaled deep enough that radical sting could clean out my brain with a *swish.*

The shower water turned brown when I rinsed out the dye, a rusty brown like dried-up blood. Peering down at it gave me vertigo. My knees wobbled. I turned the tap off and wrapped myself in a towel. Then the towel, once a pure vanilla white, was smudged with that ghastly shade of brown. *Oops,* I thought, wrapping myself tighter. *Nothing I can do about it, so why worry?* That was the Xanax talking.

Knowing the paparazzi would be at the funeral, I

decided this could be my second chance. When they'd caught me outside Eva-Kate's arguing with Josie I had on a black hoodie and no shoes. My Kool-Aid–blue hair hadn't even been brushed. I'd looked feral and cartoonish. This time, I promised to nobody in particular, it would be different.

I spent an hour blow-drying, dragging the dryer through my hair following the curve of a conical brush until my newly bronze sugar hair hung in soft but structured waves. I don't know how long I stood there staring at my reflection; it could have been a minute, it could have been hours.

I became transfixed, examining the brutal myriad of my flaws. Up close in the foggy glass my pores looked cavernous. I imagined ants crawling across my face and getting stuck. The scars from long-gone zits left a discolored trail along my left jaw. I found milia spreading on the skin around my eyes, dead cells clumped together to form little white dots like sentences in braille. *Inadequate*, they read.

I locked the door and unearthed my mother's supply of makeup from drawers beneath the marble counter. Rejects, I assumed, otherwise they would've gone along for the vacation. I smoothed Clinique Buttermilk liquid foundation over every inch of my face and blotted it with Lancôme Translucence setting powder. I looked like a ghost. I dabbed Laura Mercier Pink Rose blush onto my cheekbones. Then I looked like a clown. Hot tears sprang to my eyes.

A knock on the bathroom door made me jump.

"Justine, are you in there?"

"Yeah, uh, one minute." I shuffled the makeup back into the drawers and shoved the stained towel into the sink base cabinet, then pulled my bathrobe on and unlocked the door.

"What's wrong?" my mother asked when she saw my face. I didn't know if she was referring to my tears or to the frightening makeup job I'd done on myself. It could have been either. Or both. I cried harder then. I couldn't stop.

"I look awful," I gasped between sobs. "I can't believe this is what I look like."

"Honey, *honey*." She snatched two tissues from a box with a practiced flick of her wrist, used them to wipe my tears. "It's fine, we'll just take it off."

She meant the makeup, but it was my face I wanted off. She unscrewed a jar of Pond's Cold Cream, appraising me out of the corner of one eye.

"I don't have anything to wear to the funeral," I sniffed, realizing anything cute I owned was now lost to the crime scene of Eva-Kate's mansion. I let her clean my face. I didn't have it in me to resist, especially not with the sunny Xanax buzz settling in.

"That's ridiculous. Wear the black velvet dress Aunt Jillian got you."

"That dress is from Old Navy," I said, my voice becoming hollow and a little dazed. "I'm not wearing Old Navy to Eva-Kate Kelly's funeral."

"Nobody will be able to tell where it's from, Justine." I laughed.

"Right," I said, "influencers in couture can *never* spot low-quality off-the-rack."

She just didn't see me as part of that world. The last time she saw me I was in Gap jeans and angst-graffitied Converse. To her I was still the girl kept outside while she mingled with A-listers, tending to them like potted plants. Maybe she wanted that world to herself, but soon she'd see it was too late for that, that I'd infiltrated and been gifted my own territory. The hair on my arms bristled.

"Maybe I have something," she said. "But it would probably be too big on you."

"Worth a try," I reluctantly admitted, knowing I didn't have any other options. I was out of time to go shopping and even if I wasn't, she'd insist on going with me. I figured the only thing worse than getting photographed at a crime scene was getting photographed with your mother.

Her closet was smaller than your average mother's, no more than fifteen square feet, dresses and pantsuits of all colors and fabrics—though mostly beige and mostly linen—wedged in tightly against each other, draped over wire hangers above a pile of shoes arranged without rhyme or reason. I sat on the bed while she rifled through the dresses and pulled one out. It was navy-blue twill, knee-length, embroidered with pink and yellow flowers with blue leaves and stems. It had a halter top and a flared skirt.

"This was a gift from a patient," she said, handing it to me. "It's Kate Spade, but I could never wear it. Just not my style."

"I guess navy is close enough to black," I said, taking it from her and holding it against my body. It looked like it would fit, even if it was a little loose and a little long.

"Thanks," I said, genuinely. "This will work."

Back in my room I slipped it off the hanger and read the label. *Kate Spede.* I smiled. *A knockoff,* I thought, *even better.* Eva-Kate did love knockoffs, after all.

✳ ✳ ✳

Eva-Kate was buried at the Hollywood Forever Cemetery on Santa Monica Boulevard just like she'd always wanted. It was in her will, along with every detail of her funeral, including who should be invited. Most seventeen-year-old girls don't have a will written up, but then most seventeen-year-old girls don't own property. Most girls aren't Eva-Kate, are they?

Right from the beginning the event was riddled with imbalances and contradictions. The guest list was tiny, while the flower arrangements were extravagant, more bouquets of white roses than there were seats in the chapel, each one resting in a Tawa vase by Humble Ceramics. There was no picture of her up front, but there was an open casket, and every guest received a one-page letter-pressed program with her name in black, looping calligraphy imprinted at the top. There was no priest or hint at religion, but a row of coin-sized crystals of all colors lined the stage for guests to place into Eva-Kate's casket as a send-off gift. The paparazzi, media, and fans were barred from entry to the cemetery but swarmed the perimeters in droves.

As soon as I walked in, my heart plummeted. Of everyone in the room, I was the only one not in black, and the only one with arms exposed. Against the crowd of black, my navy dress read as neon, and the halter tie barely covered my neck, let alone my back. I felt people looking, their glances lingering a moment too long. How had I let this happen? After all the thought I'd put into my appearance, I'd failed. My skin hummed. The fact that I had miscalculated so terribly, that I had planned and plotted and still missed the mark by so much, made me queasy.

The guests formed a long, crooked line snaking up to the front of the room where a casket lay propped open, Eva-Kate's corpse resting inside. The casket was a glossy periwinkle, just like her car. I got in line and tried to keep to myself, dreading my turn to approach.

Josie, London, and Olivia huddled together toward the front of the line. London saw me come in and whispered to the other two, who turned to stare. I thought I saw a smirk sneak across Josie's matte red mouth.

I spotted Liza, the surviving twin, sitting in the pews, her silky blond hair tied with a black bow. She had Eva-Kate's face. It felt unfair that she could keep that beautiful face while Eva-Kate had to give it up. Next to her was a middle-aged woman wearing a dress too small for her voluptuous frame, breasts spilling out like two overstuffed goose-down pillows. But when it came to her face, the resemblance was unmissable. She was Liza's mother. And, therefore, Eva-Kate's mother too. Debbie McKelvoy. Even from far away I could tell she'd drugged herself for the occasion. Her body had that blissfully limp slump you get from taking a little bit too much Valium. I wanted to go back in time and do more to take the edge off.

To distract myself I counted the famous faces. Dove Cameron, Jennifer Lawrence, Bella Thorne, Millie Bobby Brown, Finn Wolfhard, Miley Cyrus, Emma Roberts, Emma Watson, Emma Stone, Ezra Miller, Camilla Belle, Joe Jonas. It was a game of I Spy I played with myself. Then there was the older generation, the actors who had either played Eva-Kate's parents or had themselves grown up in child stardom: Drew Barrymore, Brooke

Shields, Natalie Portman, Reese Witherspoon, Jodie Foster. They had escaped, but she never would.

Ruby showed up alone, without her boys, wearing a black velvet gown. I glanced back at the door three or four times, checking to see if Rob would show. He never did.

When it was my turn to see her, I held my breath. My fingers curled up involuntarily like two frightened roly-polys. Her skin was so white, a heavy magenta gloss melted onto her lips, and a holographic iridescence brushed onto her high cheekbones. Shocking blue powder settled on her closed eyelids. She wore a Juicy jumpsuit encrusted with hundreds of Swarovski crystals. She'd been bidding for it on eBay, I remembered, the Juicy suit that cost twenty-five thousand dollars. I liked knowing that she'd won it in the end. It was just like Eva-Kate to be even cooler, more victorious, dead than she'd been alive.

"We're gathered here today to remember the life of Eva-Kate Kelly," said a woman who'd appeared at the podium. She wore a long black dress that trailed to the floor, with loose, bell-shaped sleeves. She had tattoos and rings on every finger. "And what a life it was."

Nods of agreement bobbed through the room. I heard the heavy chapel doors clang shut behind me.

"My name is Frances Joy," the woman went on, her voice airy and soft and too sweet. "I had the pleasure of knowing Eva-Kate through our friend Ruby Jones. I only knew her for a year, but in that time, watching her grow and cultivate her own spiritual practice was one of the most beautiful things I've yet to witness. It is a great honor and privilege to have been asked to lead this service here with you today. Eva-Kate, both in life and death, was a young woman who knew what she wanted, and she has asked that we begin her memorial by reciting the following poem by Edgar Allan Poe. It's printed in your programs so that you can follow along."

Frances Joy was too old to be a *friend* of Eva-Kate's. I couldn't tell exactly how old, but by the way her skin was just losing some of its elasticity, I put her in her mid-forties. If Ruby was Eva-Kate's "crystal healer" and "spiritual adviser," then Frances must have been Ruby's. As far as I knew, no healing had been done. And now, in Eva-Kate's case, nor could it ever. I closed my eyes as Frances Joy's effervescent voice poured over the words like water over rocks:

> It was many and many a year ago,
> In a kingdom by the sea,
> That a maiden there lived whom you may
>   know
> By the name of Annabel Lee;
> And this maiden she lived with no other
>   thought
> Than to love and be loved by me.

I *was a child and* she *was a child,*
In this kingdom by the sea,
But we loved with a love that was more than
        love—
I and my Annabel Lee—
With a love that the wingèd seraphs of Heaven
Coveted her and me.

And this was the reason that, long ago,
In this kingdom by the sea,
A wind blew out of a cloud, chilling
My beautiful Annabel Lee;
So that her highborn kinsmen came
And bore her away from me,
To shut her up in a sepulchre
In this kingdom by the sea.

The angels, not half so happy in Heaven,
Went envying her and me—
Yes!—that was the reason (as all men know,
In this kingdom by the sea)
That the wind came out of the cloud by night,
Chilling and killing my Annabel Lee.

But our love it was stronger by far than
        the love
Of those who were older than we—
Of many far wiser than we—

And neither the angels in Heaven above
Nor the demons down under the sea
Can ever dissever my soul from the soul
Of the beautiful Annabel Lee;

For the moon never beams, without bringing
me dreams
Of the beautiful Annabel Lee;
And the stars never rise, but I feel the bright
eyes
Of the beautiful Annabel Lee;
And so, all the night-tide, I lie down by the
side
Of my darling—my darling—my life and my
bride,
In the sepulchre there by the sea—
In her tomb by the sounding sea.

At the last word, Debbie McKelvoy let out the ago-
nized wail of a small hunted animal. She jumped up
and hurried out the back doors, Liza chasing closely
after her. Others, too, started to cry, though they kept
it light, dabbing their eyes with the corners of sleeves. I
thought I should be crying too, but I couldn't. I thought
about Annabel. Had I told Eva-Kate about her? I raced
back through my memories and found electric-purple
and black smudges where conversations should have
been. I wanted to search the document of my time with

Eva-Kate for mention of the name Annabel, but there had been too much drinking, too much Xanax, too much enchantment. That combination fogged the page. Had I told her about Annabel? Had I? Was this some kind of message?

Oh, Justine. I put one hand to my cheek. *You're losing it. Grief can cause you to imagine things*, I told myself. *Your brain is grappling to make sense out of something that will never make sense.*

Frances Joy hung her head, eyes closed and hands clasped, for several moments, then breathed herself back upright.

"And now we'll hear from Josie Bishop," she said. "A lifelong friend and confidant of Eva-Kate's."

With encouraging squeezes from London and Olivia, Josie made her way to the podium, a folded-up piece of paper clutched tightly in her hand. She wore a black silk formfitting midi dress with matching gloves and the same absurdly large tortoiseshell sunglasses she'd had on the last time I'd seen her. Eva-Kate's death had already taken pounds off Josie's body. She looked like a widow. How chic, I thought, to be a young widow.

"I met Eva-Kate when we were four years old," she sniffed, reading from her paper. "Before *Jennie and Jenny.* My parents moved into the house next to her parents, and we were the only kids on the block. Me, her, and Liza. Right from the beginning she was always the assertive one, you know, the kid who makes all the rules." She paused for a weak wave of laughter from the audience. "When we were five or six we'd get together and pretend to be the Spice Girls, even though there were only three of us. Eva-Kate insisted on being Baby Spice each time; she insisted I be Ginger and Liza be Posh. We didn't have anybody to be the Melanies, but Eva-Kate always said nobody cared about the Melanies anyway. We were so young, but she would choreograph these really elaborate and impressive dances for us to do, and she'd write scripts for us too and then direct us in these little plays. We weren't allowed to take a break until we got it all down just right." She forced a small, girlish laugh. "It might sound to you like Eva-Kate was a bossy kid, and maybe at the time I thought so too, but I don't see it that way now. Looking back, I realize she was so much more than 'bossy.' Kids are bossy, but she wasn't a kid. She never was. Instead, she was driven, she was determined, she knew what she wanted and was willing to work hard to get it, even at five years old. Even at five years old she demanded the respect she knew she deserved, and she carried herself with the confidence of a seasoned boss. That confidence stayed with her until her last day on this planet. As some of you know, this funeral was planned by Eva-Kate herself. Now, I know that may sound morbid, but I think it's spectacular. I think it's a reflection of a girl completely in charge of herself. Since she was seven years old, people have been trying to take her power, but she'd never let them. She never let what anyone said change what she knew about herself, which was that she was one of a kind and heaven-sent, capable of achieving anything that she set her mind to."

This felt scripted and dishonest—the Eva-Kate I knew didn't have that confidence or self-respect. Maybe she'd had it as a kid, but by the time she died it had been taken from her. Or she'd given it away. Of course, she wanted the world to think she felt good in her own skin and knew her worth, so she'd written it out this way. Even in death, she controlled the narrative.

There was no air-conditioning in the chapel and I could feel my makeup sweating off, my heartbeat speeding up. It was getting hard to swallow. There was no end in sight for Josie's eulogy, so I quietly excused myself and leaned on the heavy chapel doors until they opened, then stumbled out into the sunlight.

The sun was too hot and the air felt dirty, filmy with car exhaust. I walked around to the side of the building where I could sit in the shade and catch my breath.

"Mom, Mom, try to calm down." Somebody was talking, but I couldn't tell where the voice was coming from. It was just like Eva-Kate's voice, only lighter and without the smoky edge. Liza.

"I can't calm down!" This must have been Debbie. "My daughter is spending eternity in a *Juicy suit*. What is this, some kind of joke?"

"Ms. McKelvoy," said a third voice, a man's. "I can assure you this is what Eva-Kate wanted, we have it all written down in the prepaid documents."

"Get those out of my face," Debbie bit back. "Why would she do this, Liza? Did she know she was going to die? Who plans their own funeral, *who does that*?"

"From what I understand, Miss Kelly had recently purchased a home?" the man said, adding a generous inflection at the end that made his statement a question, inviting Debbie into what she was otherwise barred from.

"Yes," Liza said. "That's right."

"So what?" Debbie asked. "What's your point, Mr. Ellis?"

"When she bought her house, she also wrote up a will. She didn't have to plan out her funeral in such detail, but some people find comfort in it."

"She didn't find comfort in it, she just saw one last way to torture me and took advantage of it."

"Mom, it's just a Juicy suit, okay?" Liza tried in a soothing tone. "This isn't personal."

"*Of course it's personal.* She knew how much I hated those things. So tacky. And her makeup! She looks like a hooker—and not a very good one. Doesn't a mother get a say in all this?"

Silence. The sound of papers shuffling. Delicate knuckles cracking.

"Not if Miss Kelly was an emancipated minor," Mr. Ellis said finally.

More silence. A light breeze. The whir of a lawn mower slicing through grass.

"You're judging me, Mr. Ellis," Debbie said. "I can see that you're judging me. But don't. You have no idea how difficult that girl was. An impossible creature from the day she was born. A pure nightmare, Mr. Ellis. Do you understand?"

"Mom, stop," Liza pleaded. "Not now."

"She tells people I was stealing her money? Bullshit. She has the world wrapped around her finger, even now. The true story, you wanna know the true story?"

"No, Ms. McKelvoy," said Mr. Ellis. "That's not my business."

Yes, I thought, *tell me the true story.*

"We were *broke*," she spat out. "Eva-Kate was a multimillionaire and we were broke, but she wouldn't give us a penny. And when we wanted to borrow some from her just to stay afloat, she emancipated. Do you understand what that means? She fired her family for wanting to borrow some cash. What did she need it for, Mr. Ellis? She was only fourteen; what did she need ten million dollars for?"

"Like I said, Ms. McKelvoy, it's none of my business."

"Well, maybe it should be," Debbie huffed. "Come on, Liza, it's so hot I could faint."

Next thing I knew their footsteps were coming around the corner, headed toward me. I jumped up and pretended to be taking a phone call. They brushed past me like I was invisible, Liza gripping tenaciously on to her mother's arm, practically holding her up as they walked. *Why wasn't Eva-Kate willing to lend them some money?* I wondered, standing in the cloud of dust they'd kicked up. And was Debbie telling the truth, or was this just the version of the story she wanted told? There are countless sides to every story and most people, I've found, want to tell the version in which they're the victim or the hero. Nothing in between.

I wanted to leave, to take a hot bath and drink cold whiskey. I wanted to fill the bath with whiskey and lie in it. But I stayed. I stayed so I could see her lowered into the ground. I needed the proof that she was truly gone, otherwise I'd go the rest of my life not really believing it.

✳ ✳ ✳

The periwinkle-lacquered casket descended so slowly the movement was almost imperceptible to the human eye. It was attached to one of those mechanical devices designed to make the process more pleasant, but I couldn't think of anything more awful. An elevator of death savoring every moment it took to pull her away from me. I wanted to sever the cables, to make it quick.

As the coffin lowered, Frances Joy read "Requiescat,"

a poem by Oscar Wilde. It was a creepy poem, made twice as creepy by the fact that Eva-Kate herself had planned for it to be read.

> Tread lightly, she is near
> Under the snow,
> Speak gently, she can hear
> The daisies grow.
>
> All her bright golden hair
> Tarnished with rust,
> She that was young and fair
> Fallen to dust.
>
> Lily-like, white as snow,
> She hardly knew
> She was a woman, so
> Sweetly she grew.
>
> Coffin-board, heavy stone,
> Lie on her breast,
> I vex my heart alone,
> She is at rest.
>
> Peace, Peace, she cannot hear
> Lyre or sonnet,
> All my life's buried here,
> Heap earth upon it.

"Do they have any idea who did this to her yet?" a woman standing in front of me whispered to the man standing next to her.

"Isn't it obvious?" He shrugged.

"Um . . . no?"

"She did it to herself."

"*Shut up*," the woman hissed. I seconded the sentiment.

"Think about it," he urged. "Boyfriend dumped her to date her sister. Her career's been kind of over for a while. What else was left?"

"That's not a reason to kill yourself."

"Maybe not. But then look at this funeral. She planned the whole thing! She's just a kid; why plan a funeral if she didn't know she was going to die?"

"Still. Doesn't mean she killed herself. Maybe she just knew she was going to die."

"You mean she knew somebody was going to kill her?"

"Maybe." She shrugged. He shrugged a reply, then they both went back to staring ahead, waiting for the casket to finally dip out of sight as if they were watching a sunset, as if they had all the time in the world.

I had made up my mind to leave when out of the corner of my eye I saw Rob's tall, hunched figure swaying and swaggering over to where we stood. He found a tree, leaned his full weight onto it, then slid down with his back against the flaky bark and lit a cigarette. I had to laugh. He was like a cartoon. The enemy of discretion. He wore grass-stained jeans and a white T-shirt torn at the neck; his face had the red puffiness of a drunk's. Sure enough, he pulled a flask from his back pocket and held the cigarette between his teeth as he unscrewed it. Then he dropped the cigarette and took a sip, snatching the cigarette back up just as a blade of grass was catching fire, stomping clumsily on the blade until the flame went out. He was bound to attract attention in a minute, and once he did there was no way I'd get a chance to talk to him.

"Rob." I crouched down to his level. "Let's get out of here."

"Hm?" His eyes were pink and glazed over. He smelled strongly of sweat and whiskey.

"You're wasted and the paparazzi are everywhere." I tried to make my voice sound official and authoritative, a voice he might take direction from. "You don't want them to get you looking like this."

"I didn't want people to think I don't care," he slurred, looking into the open flask. "So I came. But I couldn't do it sober. Could you?"

"Not really, no." I hooked my hand around the crook of his elbow and coaxed him upward. "Let's go."

"Where are we going?" To my total shock, he stood up.

"Not far," I told him, scouting out a nearby mausoleum.

It would have to work; as soon as one picture of the two of us was snapped, all bets would be off. And it could happen any second. The mausoleum had Greek-style decorative pillars and marble steps leading up to a cement-sealed door. I took his wrist and pulled him behind it.

"Can I help you?" he asked, half scowling, half giggling like a schoolboy.

"You can tell me where you were the night Eva-Kate died," I said, releasing his wrist.

"Oh boy." He rolled his eyes and took a drag from the cigarette. "We have a detective, do we?"

"You may not realize this," I said, "but we don't have time for witty banter. You and me, the detectives have their eyes on us, and if you don't have an alibi—"

"*Me?* Why do they have their eyes on *me?*"

"You're the boyfriend. It's almost always the—"

"*Ex-boyfriend,*" he corrected me. "And I don't have a motive."

"Maybe not an obvious one," I said, recalling the screenshots Eva-Kate was all set to release the night she died. The proof that he had gotten an underage girl pregnant. Had he known? Had she told him?

"What's that supposed to mean?" He was getting too loud.

I considered asking him about it, rolling the thought back and forth like dice, then decided against it.

"Never mind. It doesn't matter. Do you have an alibi or not?"

He paused for a moment and looked me up and down with a dazed smile, as if he enjoyed watching me squirm.

"Of course I do," he said finally. "I was with Liza."

"And people can vouch for that?"

"Uh, Liza can."

"Well, how convenient," I said, ripping at my cuticle.

"What, you think we *both* did something to her?"

"If she was standing in the way of you being together, sure."

"Fuck, Justine, you're so far off. She *wasn't* standing in the way of us being together. We *were* together, we were happy. But when Eva-Kate died, Liza dumped me."

"Wait, what?"

"Yep."

"But . . . why?"

"No explanation. Just says it's too painful now." He dug the toe of his boot into the soil. "She can't be with me anymore. Won't even talk to me. Moved back in with her mom."

"She dumped you . . . *after Eva-Kate died?*"

"Yes!" he laughed bitterly. "Do we have to keep talking about it?"

"No, I'm just trying to . . ." *I'm just trying to figure out how she could have died,* I didn't say. *Trying to figure out why you might have killed her.*

"Rob, over here!" a man's voice hollered, followed by the ballistic snapping of a camera and the accompanying bursts of light.

They found us. I shielded my face from the flashing bulbs that multiplied from one to dozens in an impressive few seconds. They must have been hiding out in plain sight, slipping through the trees, disguised as civilian mourners casually passing through.

Rob, did you do it FLASH Rob, where's Liza FLASH did she help you do it FLASH why are you with Justine FLASH are you together FLASH Justine, do you think he did it FLASH what are you wearing FLASH why'd you kill her FLASH FLASH why'd you do it FLASH FLASH Rob, how much have you had to drink FLASH FLASH FLASH do you miss her yet FLASH FLASH FLASH FLASH FLASH!

Through the blinding splotches I saw Rob put out his cigarette and light a new one, calm and cavalier as if alone in the privacy of his own bedroom. I put my hands up to shield my face and tried to slip away like I had that day outside Eva-Kate's, but this time they followed. As my footsteps quickened, so did theirs, the questions getting louder with every step. These were grown men, and I was no athlete, there was no way I could outrun them. Disoriented by the lights, I couldn't see any way out. I tripped on a rock and fell, scraping my knee. I burst into tears.

Then there were hands on my shoulders. Warm, strong, unexpected.

"Run." It was Rob's voice in my ear. "I'll take them from here."

I looked up at his face, urging me to go, and I ran.

CHAPTER 5

ROB DONOVAN COMFORTS A HYSTERICAL JUSTINE CHILDS

I drank myself to sleep and woke up feeling like I'd been hit by a truck. My head pounded, my bones ached, the room spun. My knee still bled. Memories of the funeral were foggy and felt a lifetime away. There was a smoke screen between then and now, making the whole thing feel like it had taken place in another dimension. I found the hand-me-down iPhone 5 at the foot of my bed, swiped it on, and typed "Eva-Kate Kelly funeral" into the search engine.

NEW ROMANCE? ROB DONOVAN EMBRACES JUSTINE CHILDS AT HOLLYWOOD FOREVER CEMETERY

It sat among the other headlines like a tombstone. I whimpered. This was so much worse than I'd imagined.

The pictures portrayed Rob and me as distorted versions of ourselves. With his arms around me he looked nurturing and sober, almost fatherly. One picture was a zoomed-in close-up of my wet, red face with the caption: "ROB DONOVAN COMFORTS A HYSTERICAL JUSTINE CHILDS."

Why *had* he helped me? He'd flicked his cigarette at the cameras and given me an escape route. It was a decent thing to do and made me wonder if he *was* decent. The thought itself felt like a betrayal of Eva-Kate. I shook it off. *He knew she was going to release the text messages and so he killed her before she could do it,* I told myself. I just needed proof.

You always hear the loved ones of murder victims talk about needing to find out who killed them, needing to see the killer brought to justice. I never understood. Knowing who killed them, seeing that person pay for what they'd done, none of that brings back what was taken from you, so why bother? Now I understand. Not knowing what happened to Eva-Kate felt like a screaming itch deep in my skin that nothing could silence. I hoped answers would at least quiet the scream. If Liza could confirm that Rob wasn't with her that night, prove that he was lying, then he wouldn't have an alibi. And if I told the detectives about the texts he was afraid of getting out, then he'd have a motive.

I remembered that day at the Madonna Inn. Eva-Kate had said that if she ever wanted to break up Rob and Liza, all she had to do was show Liza the texts. Maybe she did show her and maybe Liza dumped him because of them. Maybe Rob went to Eva-Kate's house to confront her about it, and maybe things got out of control. It made all the sense in the world. I just needed to hear it from Liza.

She can't be with me anymore. Won't even talk to me. Moved back in with her mom.

Rob's slurred, jilted words bubbled up in my mind just as I needed them to. If I was looking for Liza, there was a good chance I'd find her at her mom's house. Wherever the fuck that was. Burbank? Chatsworth? Eva-Kate had told me once, but all I could remember was that it was in the Valley. Somewhere that got up to 110 degrees in the summer and adult toy stores littered the boulevards. Somewhere I preferred not to go.

Down the hall I could hear my mother's phone ring, that upbeat synthetic steel drum jingle with a spring in its step.

"This is Dr. Nancy Childs," she answered, the same way she'd been doing for as long as I could remember. "How can I help?"

For a moment, the weight of my hangover lifted. I knew how I'd get to Liza.

* * *

While she was on the phone, I snuck into my mom's office. A part of me was expecting the file cabinet to be gone, but it was still there. I was expecting the combination would have been changed, but when I pressed it into the keypad, the drawers clicked open. The McKelvoy file was just where I'd left it. I opened it to the first page and sure enough, there on the intake form from Eva-Kate's first session was an address: 55 Vanalden Ave, Reseda, California. I took a photo on my phone and stuffed the papers back into their drawer, then slammed it shut. I could only hope the McKelvoys hadn't moved.

It was forty-eight hours later when I finally found the courage to go see Liza. I waited until my mom had three patients back to back, then used my mom's hand-me-down iPhone 5 and my debit card to call an Uber. I put half a milligram of Xanax under my tongue to keep my nerves down on the long drive to Reseda.

The house on Vanalden Ave was the gray green of an old avocado's insides, one story with a low-hanging gable roof and an overgrown oak tree casting shade over the whole property. The 101 freeway ran over the backyard. I forced myself up the front path, keeping my eyes down, watching my shadow pass over the cracks in the pavement, half hoping no one was home.

I rang the doorbell. When a minute went by without a response, I rang it again.

This time Liza came to the door, looking distraught and caught off guard. I was startled too; there's no way to prepare yourself for seeing a dead girl's face restored to life right before your eyes. Up close Liza was an almost identical replica of her sister, an alternate Eva-Kate Kelly with self-cut bangs, clear-framed glasses, and no makeup on. I knew I was staring but I couldn't stop.

"Yes?" she asked, "Can I help you?" She wore jean shorts and a T-shirt. The room behind her smelled like cats and dust and maybe mold hidden deep in the walls.

"Hi," I said, awkwardly extending my hand. "I don't think we've met. I'm Justine. I was a friend of your sister's."

"Liza," she said, shaking my hand. "Good to meet you."

"I . . . I'm really sorry for your loss," I said, getting quiet when I realized I hadn't planned what I'd say.

"Yeah, well," she said, looking me right in the eyes. "If you were her friend, then it was more your loss than mine. I lost her a very long time ago."

I was disarmed by how she could look so much like her sister but act so differently. She was straightforward, without a motive or a mission slithering beneath her words. With no makeup and very little jewelry, she looked so wholesome, uncorrupted, like the kind of girl who's into horses or science and has somehow, by some miracle, managed to develop a sense of self-worth independent of other people's opinions. She wasn't putting on a show, and I didn't have to try to read her mind, because it was very clear just from her body language what she wanted: for me to leave and let her go back to grieving in peace. Or maybe I was projecting.

"Yeah," I said, my head starting to hurt from clenching my jaw too tightly. "I'm sorry about that too."

"Don't be ridiculous." She smiled kindly. "That's not your fault. Was there . . . something you wanted to talk about? You didn't come all the way out here to give me your condolences, did you?"

"I wanted to ask you about the night Eva-Kate died," I blurted before I could change my mind. I knew if I hesitated I'd lose my nerve and go home without anything I came for. "And about Rob."

"Why?" She crossed her arms. Not defensively, but with genuine confusion.

"*Why?*" I didn't understand the question. "I just want to know what happ—"

"Sorry, I didn't say that right." She put a soft, reassuring hand on my forearm. "Of course we all want to know what happened. But why you? This doesn't have to be your job. Go home, take a nap; you look exhausted. And I can say that because I look exhausted too. *I am exhausted.* I haven't slept since she died, and I haven't gotten anyone to cover my shifts, so I'm basically running on coffee and anxiety. I'm gonna try to rest and I think you should too."

"I wish I could take a nap, believe me, but . . ."

"But what?"

"I can't sleep either. Not knowing what happened to her."

She took pity on me then.

"Okay." She peered back into the house, then closed the door so that she was standing with me out on the front steps. "My stepdad is sleeping and if my mom knows I'm talking to anyone about Eva-Kate she'll flip out. Let's go to the tree house."

I followed her to the corner of the yard where a red wooden box was nestled into the branches of an oak tree. Eva-Kate had never mentioned her stepdad. I wondered why, and if somehow it was relevant.

"I helped Billy build this when we were nine," she said, resting her hand on the rope ladder that hung down from the tree house.

"Billy?"

"Oh, Billy McKelvoy, my stepdad."

"You and Eva-Kate have your stepdad's last name?" I asked, and regretted it immediately. "I'm sorry, that's a stupid question. And none of my business. Ignore me."

"Doesn't seem like a stupid question to me," she said. "Our birth father left the picture before we were born. I don't even know who he is. Billy married my mom when we were three, so we all took his last name."

"Got it." I forced myself to smile. "But I interrupted you. You were saying you built this tree house . . ."

"Right, yeah. Billy and I built it one summer when Evelyn was away filming the *Jennie and Jenny* Halloween special in Santa Barbara. Do you remember that episode? The old bank was scheduled for demolition, and Jenny the grandmother spirit locked Jennie the girl in a vault to teach her a lesson about not taking life's comforts for granted. Then of course it was Halloween so the vault was haunted by the ghosts of bank heist casualties. It was kinda fucked up for a kids' show."

"I remember it," I said.

"Scared the living daylights out of me," she said. "Especially the ghost with half his head blown off. But I guess kids are tougher these days."

"It scared me too," I told her. "I had nightmares that I was trapped down there by my parents. They just wanted to give me a quick time-out but then they forgot about me. They forgot the building was gonna blow up."

"I had thousands of those nightmares," she told me. "My entire life was that nightmare."

She started climbing up the ladder, scurrying easily to the top. I didn't particularly want to be in such a closed space with Liza McKelvoy. All I knew about her was that she'd stolen her sister's boyfriend and was suspiciously sweet. She looked like she'd strolled right out of *Sheltered Honor Student Magazine. Beautiful, Crushworthy, Sheltered Honor Student Magazine.* But I climbed up after her, deciding I'd go much stranger places with her than a tree house if it meant I could get a better idea of what happened to Eva-Kate that night, or at least gain the confidence that Liza herself shouldn't be a suspect.

"We carved our names into the wood here." She traced the letters spelling *Evelyn Kathleen* with her finger. "Not together, though; we never came up here at the same time."

"Does that make you sad?"

"It didn't used to," she said. "But now that she's gone, yeah, it does a little."

"What happened to make you . . . I mean, did you always . . . hate each other?"

"No, I didn't hate her. She hated me."

"Can I . . . ask you why?"

Liza hesitated. Then sighed and said, "You know, I'm not really sure when it started. She always felt that our mom loved me more than she loved her, and she resented me for it."

"Was she right? Did your mom really love you more?"

"Yes," she said, without missing a beat. "And I'm not surprised Eva-Kate could tell. Mom was never good to her; they had an . . . unfortunate relationship."

"Oh."

"And the hardest part for her was that she did everything my mom wanted. Everything Eva-Kate did was to get our mom's love. But I did things my own way and had her love without ever trying. My mom had wanted us to be on TV ever since we were four . . . maybe even three years old. Eva-Kate thrived in front of the camera, and I hated it more than anything. I fought it every step of the way, while she ate it all up, filled herself up with it until it was all she was. But still, she pursued my mom's love while my mom gave it all to me. And of course, I didn't want it. All I wanted was for her to love Eva-Kate, so that Eva-Kate would stop hating me."

"I'm sorry," I said. "That's really fucked up."

"That wasn't even the bad part. That came later, when we'd been on *Jennie and Jenny* for a year and the producers decided they only needed to use one of us to play the role now that we were old enough to work extra hours."

"So then you dropped out, right?"

"Wasn't as simple as that. They wanted me to stay and her to leave."

"Oh God." I felt a twinge of sympathy pain for Eva-Kate, a sour edge cutting into my sternum. "Poor Eva-Kate."

"She was the one who wanted it, and I was the one who wanted out. I had to beg them to choose her over me. I had to tell them I refused, so that their only options were her or nobody. They gave her the role, but she could never forget that they'd wanted me instead. It drove her crazy. I don't think she ever got over it."

"Do you think . . . I mean, could she have . . . done this to herself?"

"Suicide? Doubtful. She was the anti-suicide poster girl, remember?"

"Sure. But . . . when Rob left her . . . could it have triggered something . . . dark?"

Liza looked out the tree house window and was quiet for a moment. When she looked back at me her eyes were wet.

"Maybe." She shifted her position. "Maybe she was doing drugs again. Was she?"

"Was she doing *drugs*?" I repeated the question, not understanding how she could be that naive. It was Hollywood. And Eva-Kate was a teenage millionaire.

"I'm not an idiot." She read my mind. "I know she, like, *did drugs*. But I mean, was she back on painkillers? Opiates."

"Oh, I don't know. I didn't know she had a problem with those."

"She was always able to keep it out of the news. I just assumed she told you."

"No, she didn't. But she died from a knife wound, not an overdose."

"Yeah, but maybe it was drug *related*. Like, maybe she was caught up in something. Something that went wrong." She laughed sadly. "Listen to me, I watch too many movies."

"I talked to Rob after the funeral," I told her. "He said he was with you the night she died. Is that true?"

Her left eye twitched slightly.

"Yeah," she said. "He was."

"Are you sure?"

"Of course I'm sure! We were together almost all the time. We were at his condo all night, you can probably confirm that with the doorman. Why do you think he would kill her? It doesn't even make sense."

"Because of the texts." I took a chance. "She wanted to break you up, so she showed them to you and you dumped him. He was furious. So he killed her."

"Excuse me?" she laughed. "*That's* your theory?"

"Kind of. Maybe." I shrugged, second-guessing.

"You're talking about the texts between him and Carolyn?"

"Is that the girl he—"

"Got pregnant. Yes. Carolyn Carr. I've known about those texts for a long time, Justine. I've known the whole story."

"*You have? How?* Eva-Kate said if you ever found out you'd leave him. She said you would never be okay with it."

"Goes to show how much she knew about me. Rob told me what happened even before we started dating. He didn't want me to find out from someone else. Of course I was upset, but honesty means everything to me."

"So then why did you break up with him?"

"Because he hurt Eva-Kate, and I love her. He didn't kill her, but he broke her heart, and I hate that I was a part of that in any way. When she died I just looked at him and realized he'd never stop making me feel guilty. I still love him, but . . . it's hard to explain. It has to be over, at least for now."

"Okay, okay, right." I thought quickly, my mind working overtime for answers. "So you knew about the texts, but Eva-Kate was going to release them to the public, and that would ruin his career. That's a motive right there."

"Justine." She wiped her eyes. "He *wanted* his career to be over. He's wanted a way out forever."

"Sure, but it's not just his career; if the story got out it would ruin his reputation. For life. Even *after* life . . . it would fuck with his legacy. Forever."

"Would it really? They were both under eighteen. Celebrities have been forgiven for a lot worse."

"Maybe . . ." She had a point.

"It doesn't really matter," she said. "Because he was with me. All night. The detectives will clear him as a suspect as soon as they confirm that with the building. If they haven't already."

"Okay," I sighed, conceding. "Yeah, okay. I'm sorry I took up so much of your time. Thanks for your help."

"I wish I had more to tell you," she said, climbing back out onto the rope ladder. "And I'm sorry I couldn't give you what you wanted."

"No," I said, following her down. "It helps to know Rob was telling the truth. And it helps to know you didn't hate your sister."

"I didn't," she said, shielding her eyes from the sun. "I miss her a lot."

As her hand rose up over her eyes, I caught a flash of the inside of her upper arm, smooth white flesh that peeked out when her sleeve fell back. There was a design tattooed onto it, delicate lines forming a brief squiggle. I wouldn't have known what it was if I hadn't seen it before on both Rob and Zander: VWWL.

"Can I ask you one more question?"

"Sure." She squinted.

"What's that tattoo on your arm? I saw it on Rob. Does it mean anything?"

"No," she said quickly, blushing. "It's just a design."

"You got matching tattoos?"

"Yep."

"Then why does Zander have it too?"

"You know Zander?" Her blush darkened.

"I've met him," I said. "So are you three in some kind of polyamorous triad?"

"I really can't talk about this," she said. "You should probably go now."

"Liza, please," I begged, "help me find out who did this. If the tattoo has nothing to do with it, just tell me. Just tell me I'm wrong."

She adjusted her glasses, eyes roving the sky, then the browning blades of grass.

"Fine," she agreed finally. "The athame, did Eva-Kate ever tell you who gave it to her?"

"She said your mom did. That she had a penchant for the occult, and—"

"*My mom?*" she laughed. "Eva-Kate really said that? God, she was something else. No, it was a gift from Ruby."

"Ruby Jones? The crystal healer?"

"Crystal healer by day," she corrected me. "Something else entirely by night."

"What is she by night?"

"She's a hustler, that's what. She rules her own little kingdom and she's ruthless about it."

"How so? What do you mean by—"

"Justine, you cannot tell anyone you heard this from me, okay?"

"Yes, yes, okay, of course. What is it?"

"The tattoo is a ticket into a very exclusive club. With membership you have access to the best parties in Los Angeles, you get to mingle with the best agents and casting directors, you get the best drugs if you want them. When you're in with Underworld, you're in the center of everything. You're as elite as it can get."

"*Underworld?* Why have I never heard of it?"

She laughed. "Underworld Wonderland. Nobody's heard of it who isn't *in* it."

"So, like, the first rule of Underworld Wonderland is don't talk about Underworld Wonderland?" I joked.

"Pretty much," she replied with a straight face, not joking.

"Oh." I was lost and that old feeling was coming back, the feeling of being hopelessly on the outside. "And Eva-Kate was a member?"

Liza nodded. "Ruby's dad was an original member from 1979 and now she's in charge of who's in and who's out."

And why were you in? She was the girl who supposedly wanted nothing to do with the Hollywood scene.

"And you think . . . what exactly?"

"I think Ruby is psycho," she said. "And if you've met

Zander and her other boys then you know there's something really off there."

"So, you mean—"

"I've already said way too much, Justine." She put her hands up apologetically. "If you want more, you'll have to talk to Ruby herself."

CHAPTER 6

JUSTINE CHILDS SEARCHES FOR ANSWERS

The next day, a Tuesday, was pleasantly drizzly. My Uber driver's name was Fabrina and she blasted Jay-Z and Kanye West's *Watch the Throne* as we headed back down the 405 and onto the 5, riding along the beach. Yes, that's Fabrina, like Sabrina but with an *F*. The digital clock in her silver Honda Civic said it was noon.

I'd briefly considered going to the police with my new information, but I knew all along that I wouldn't. What would I have told them? That I thought Rob Donovan might have murdered Eva-Kate Kelly because she was blackmailing him with text screenshots? Or that maybe it was the resentful sister who shot the messenger when Eva-Kate showed her said screenshots? Both were semi-decent theories, but I had nothing to back either up, and according to Liza there was proof to corroborate their alibis. So I'd move on to Ruby. What did it mean to be a hustler? A ruthless ruler of her own kingdom? Had she really given that athame to Eva-Kate? When they tested it for fingerprints, would they find hers?

I didn't have Ruby's address, but when Fabrina got off the freeway in San Onofre I was able to guide her to the beach house Eva-Kate had taken me to that day. It was easy: two lefts then a right, then a left again, no more than half a mile from the freeway. The nuclear power plant loomed, two bulbous tumors growing up out of the beach.

When I knocked on Ruby's front door, Declan appeared, topless, as he was last time, but this time with red eyes. Was he her butler? Who were these boys to her?

"Cobalts or Crimsons?" he asked when he saw me there, rubbing his eyes.

"Sorry, what?"

"Going up or down?"

"Umm?"

"Are you looking to go up?" He pointed theatrically to the sky. "Or are you looking to go down?" He spiraled his finger toward the ground with a goofy, crooked-toothed grin.

"I'm looking for Ruby Jones," I said, annoyed at myself for choosing such a formal tone.

"Oh, yikes." He made a wincing, sour face. "Nobody who really knows her calls her that. Anyone showing up here calling her Jones is surely not here for any of the reasons we like to have people here."

"I . . . don't understand."

"It doesn't matter." He got serious then. "She's not here."

"Are you just saying that because I didn't call her the right name?"

"I am saying it because you didn't call her the right name, but I'm also saying it because she's not here."

"Can you tell me where I could find her?"

"Ha," he said. "Yeah right. You don't know what to call her and you had no idea what I meant by going up or down; for all I know you could be a cop."

"Me?" I balked. "Have you seen me?"

"There are plenty of undercover cops who look twelve."

"I'm *sixteen*," I said. "And I'm not a cop. But why would you care if I was? Is something illegal going on?"

It was a dumb move, but I was offended and getting impatient. The feeling of being locked out made my heart race.

"All right, we're done here." He started closing the door on me.

"No, wait." I held it open with my arm. "It's about Eva-Kate."

"What about her?"

"I'm trying to find out how she died. Why she died. I thought Ruby could help me."

"Wait, are you that girl who was living with Eva-Kate?"

"Yes. Why?"

"Whoa. You're not even gonna believe this, but Ruby was actually looking for you."

"Do you know why?"

"She thinks you can help *her* find out what happened. Seems like you two should be sharing info or whatever."

"Then can you tell me where she is?"

"I don't know where she is right now, but I do know tonight she'll be at Je Vous En Prie."

"Je Vou . . . ?"

"The club?"

"Amazing, thank you."

"But you won't be able to get in unless you're one of us."

"One of who?"

He flashed his wrist at me long enough so I could see the tattoo, then swung it back down.

"The Underworld . . ."

"Yeah, you in?"

"Mhm." I nodded.

"Then you'll have no problem. Door guy is named Saxon, just show him your tattoo."

"Right," I said, stiffening. "Got it. Thanks."

"You got it. See ya."

He saluted and slammed the door shut.

Dammit. I clenched and unclenched my fists. I didn't have the tattoo, I wouldn't get in. I knocked again and the door swung back open.

"You're not really a member, are you?" Declan smirked proudly. "Knew it," he said. Him knowing that I didn't belong made me want him dead.

"I'm only helping because I know Ruby wants to see you," he said. "And I know this is what she'd want me to do."

"Great. So . . ."

"When you see Saxon and he asks for your tattoo, tell him you're new. Then he'll ask you for the password. Tonight it's Messiah Apocalypse."

"What does that mean?" I asked, committing it to memory.

"If you have to ask, you obviously don't know."

"Of course I don't know," I said. "That's why I asked. I think you mean 'if you have to ask then you'll never know.'"

"Whatever."

"Do *you* know what it means?"

He was about to speak but then held back and sighed.

"No, no idea, couldn't care less. Spencer makes them up. Tuesdays are kind of his night. He's the resident photographer. And DJ."

"Spencer Sawyer?"

"Yep. That idiot."

"Got it." I saw a text come in from my mom and chose to ignore it, and instead looked back up at Declan and asked, "What are Cobalts and Crimsons?"

"If you have to ask"—he smiled—"then you'll never know."

✱ ✱ ✱

Saxon the doorman looked me up and down. He wore a black hoodie and on top of that a brown suede bowler hat. He was the first guy I'd ever seen successfully pull off eyeliner. I stood perfectly still like one movement could trip an invisible laser and set off an alarm.

"Tattoo?" he asked.

"I'm new," I shot back with a smile I hoped was firm but friendly.

"Password?" he went on without blinking.

"Messiah Apocalypse," I recited, summoning all the confidence I had.

Again, without blinking, without betraying the slightest emotion, he unhooked a red velvet rope and jerked his head in the direction of the door.

Walking up a set of black carpeted stairs, I could

hear music getting louder, heavy synth and heavy bass, and the sound of a hundred conversations happening at once. The first room was a Moroccan-style bar lit by the honey glow of a chandelier. On blue tufted sofas sat bare-legged girls and scruffy-faced guys, not one of them looking a day over seventeen. In "22," off her fourth album, *Red*, Taylor Swift mentions kids who're too cool to know who Taylor Swift is. I never thought people like that could possibly exist. But here they were. I found them.

Above the sofas was a mosaic made from reflective glass tiles, catching and refracting the light, casting a disco-ball glimmer onto the room. I stood by the bar and surveyed the room for Ruby's big, brassy array of curls.

"What are you having?" The bartender startled me. I turned to face her and the wall of liquor behind her, immediately feeling better with my back to the room.

"Scotch, please," I said. "Just plain. No ice."

"Oh, *really*?" She was impressed. "I like your style."

"Thanks." I smiled shyly.

"Gotta love a girl who likes it neat. Preference?"

"Preference . . . ?" I had to yell for her to hear me over the music. They were Top 40 songs, but warped and deformed by remix upon remix. In 2013, Cedric Gervais remixed Lana Del Rey's "Summertime Sadness." We were now listening to a remix of that remix.

"Type of scotch? Do you have a preference?"

"Oh." I glanced up at the top shelf. "Lagavulin 16, if you have it."

She poured me something from the top shelf and when I tried to pay for it, she held up her hand.

"Don't worry about it."

I thanked her and took a big gulp, then thanked God for the immediate release. Living in my own skin had only become more and more uncomfortable over the years, and now it was almost too much to bear. I savored any moment when that painful self-consciousness could be lifted.

✳ ✳ ✳

"Justine?" The voice behind me was high-pitched and appalled. I recognized it immediately as Olivia's, accompanied by London's unkind giggles. I turned around.

"Wow," said Olivia, holding a martini glass, maybe a little drunk, "I thought it was you, but I also thought no way could you possibly have the nerve to show your face. Guess I was wrong." The inside of her mouth was a bright, electric red like she'd downed an entire jar of maraschino cherries.

"Excuse me?" I took a step back, but was cornered by the crowd that had formed around the bar.

"Everyone knows you killed her," London cut in, popping up out of the darkened crowd. "Josie told us everything."

"Josie doesn't know what she's talking about," I assured her, trying to push past. They joined together to block my way. My heart pounded. What had Josie told them? Judging by their faith in her story, it sounded to me like she'd woven a convincing one. And who were people going to believe? Eva-Kate's personal assistant or some new girl with a questionable mental health history?

"The truth is going to come out. You might as well turn yourself in," said Olivia.

"Why, Olivia? Why would I kill her?"

"Because you were in love with her and she didn't feel the same way."

"I was *not* in love with her. This is so absurd. We barely knew each other."

"So you're saying your relationship was purely platonic?" Olivia challenged, unwrapping what looked like a small red marble and sliding it into her mouth.

I thought about how Eva-Kate had kissed me, insisting it wasn't just the alcohol. Maybe it hadn't been a dream. And there'd been a light in her eyes, a presence, making me believe she actually wasn't all that drunk, and that she knew exactly what she was doing. She'd pulled my dress off so easily, her movements so coordinated as she pushed me down onto the bed and straddled me with her silk-smooth legs.

What had happened then? I tried to remember but couldn't; the memory was so murky all I could make out were streaks of skin and hair and lips, the sound of Cigarettes After Sex on the turntable—*your lips, my lips, apocalypse*—then black. Had I fallen asleep? Blacked out? *How much did I have to drink?* I asked myself for the hundredth time since summer had begun.

"Yes," I said. "Yes, it was purely platonic."

Whatever it was, it was none of her business.

"Liv," said London, checking her purse, "I'm out of Crimsons, can I have one?"

"Fine, but you owe me." Olivia handed one of the wrapped red spheres to London.

Cobalts or Crimsons? Declan had asked me just a few hours earlier. *Are you looking to go up or are you looking to go down?* By Olivia's jittery belligerence, I gathered that Crimsons must be the way up.

"Hey," I asked, "where did you get those?"

Olivia looked down at me like I was the most pathetic creature she'd ever seen.

"As if I would tell you, ya psycho bitch." She laughed.

I flinched at those last three words. Not because they stung—though they did—but because they felt familiar. *I hope you die, ya Barbie*, someone had written on Eva-Kate's Instagram. *We're literally at the beach*, Olivia had said to London that morning at Soho Malibu, *so yeah, it does have to be bright, ya vampire.*

A shiver zigzagged up my spine. I stared at her, needing to see into her thoughts.

"Olivia," I asked, "where were *you* the night Eva-Kate died?"

She froze for a moment, clutching on to the leather strap of her Rag & Bone purse, then laughed, exposing her bloodred molars.

"Bitch, you must be kidding," she said. "I can tell you where I wasn't, and that's Eva-Kate's bedroom. You know who *was* there? You. If you think this Nancy Drew act is gonna make you look innocent, you're wrong. Once they find your fingerprints on that knife, it's all over for you, baby blue."

"Yeah," I said, "we'll see about that."

Ruby sidled up to us, manifesting from the crowd, and grabbed hold of my wrist. "Olivia, stop being a bully," she suggested calmly. "It's not a good look on you."

"Yeah, well." Olivia sipped her martini. "I'm not exactly going for *good*, now am I?"

"Couldn't possibly care less, babe. I'm gonna steal Justine for a bit, hope you don't mind."

"Couldn't possibly care less." Olivia stared daggers at me, and I stared right back at her. A personal colloquialism was not enough to prove guilt, that's for sure, but I was putting the pieces together, whether she liked it or not.

CHAPTER 7

IS THE PARTY OVER FOR JUSTINE CHILDS?

"Everyone has their own grieving process," Ruby said as she pulled me into the next room. "I wouldn't take it personally."

"She thinks I killed Eva-Kate," I said. "That's as personal as it gets."

Ruby stopped short. The room we were in now was three times the size of the first one, with red stucco walls and houndstooth lounge chairs and spiraling topiary and a canvas roof pulled to one side so that partygoers could look up at the stars and smoke.

"She thinks *you* did this?" Ruby furrowed her brow.

"That's what she says, yeah."

"What an imbecile," she said. "Here, let's go this way."

I followed her through the crowd to a second bar, this one with art deco fixtures and almost no light whatsoever. She walked around to the left of the bar and pushed open a swinging door that led to a chilly service hallway with a placard warning, EMPLOYEES ONLY.

"Are we allowed to be back here?" I asked, following her down the hall.

"You're cute," she said without stopping, her crushed-velvet dress lightly sweeping the floor. The hallway led to an aluminum staircase that went to the roof, where some bartenders and busboys were taking a cigarette break. They turned to acknowledge her, waved hello without even the smallest smile, then went back to their cigarettes and quiet conversation.

"You know them?" I asked, just trying for an icebreaker.

"I know everyone," she said, lighting a cigarette. "I'm sorry about Olivia. She's just looking for someone to blame. Plus her heart is made of ice. She's a sick girl."

I thought it strange that Eva-Kate's healer would also be a smoker. *A hustler, a ruler of her own little kingdom.*

"Sick? How sick? Do you think she could have . . . I mean, I'm sort of wondering if—"

"Could she have killed Eva-Kate?" Ruby inhaled. "Definitely not. She's a total baby around blood. One time she cut her hand on a broken champagne glass and literally fainted. Like, literally, we had to take her to the hospital. Plus, she didn't have any kind of motive whatsoever."

"Then who do you think did it?"

"Dr. Silver."

"Who the hell is that?"

"Eva-Kate's plastic surgeon. He did her lips."

"*What?* Why would *he* kill her? What makes you think it was him?"

"She ever tell you about him?"

He retired in 2012 but he's been a darling about making time for me here and there. He's the only one I trust not to fuck up my mouth.

"A little. I know he was retired and she was his only client."

"Well, not anymore. And he wasn't retired. He lost his license because of malpractice. I think he was caught operating under the influence. Then he started working illegally. You know, pretending to have a license or whatever."

"Shady."

"But now he has his license back and is working again."

"Okay . . . but why would he kill her?"

"She was going to expose him. He was obsessed with her, calling, sending weird presents. His practice is finally thriving again. I think he'd do anything to keep it."

"Why would she blackmail him?" I wondered if there was anybody she hadn't been blackmailing. "And why would she knowingly get lip injections from somebody with that kind of history? She said he was the only one she trusted to—"

"I don't totally understand it, but it was kind of her thing. Blackmail. I think she enjoyed it, feeling powerful, having control over people. When he started taking on new clients again, she got . . . possessive."

"Jesus," I whispered. "Where was he the night of the murder?"

"That's the best part. Or the worst part. London told me he came by the house. That night."

"Plastic surgeons don't generally make house calls."

"Exactly. I'd go talk to him if I were you."

"Why me?"

"I heard you've been asking around, trying to figure out what happened. This is a good lead, trust me."

"Too dangerous," I said. "If he really did kill her I can't go around accusing him."

"Don't *accuse* him, just ask some questions. I'll come with you. I'll have my boys stand guard in case anything goes wrong."

What are those boys doing for you? I wanted to ask, but thought better of it. She was helping and I didn't want to scare her away.

"Why are you helping me? I mean, thank you, but why?"

"It doesn't exactly look good that the murder weapon was a gift from me," she said. "If we don't find who really did this, I could be in trouble."

The athame. In the shuffle of Cobalts and Crimsons and passwords and remixes and Olivia becoming my newest suspect, I'd forgotten why I'd come looking for Ruby in the first place: Liza had said the athame was a gift from Ruby. And now Ruby had confirmed it.

"How did they know? I mean, that you're the one who gave it to her."

"They were able to trace it to my Etsy account."

"Etsy? I thought it was a medieval artifact."

"*Imitation* medieval artifact."

"Of course," I said, allowing myself a brief moment of amusement. "Wait, but then . . ."

"Then who's to say I'm not guilty?"

"Well . . ."

"I have an airtight alibi. I was still in San Luis Obispo. There are multiple witnesses who can attest to that. On top of all that, I don't have a motive. We've been friends for as long as I can remember, practically sisters. Nothing but love there."

"I have to sit down," I said. "This is all too much."

"Then sit," she said. "You don't have to ask my permission."

We sat with our backs against the chain-link barricade between the roof and the three-story drop to the street.

✷ ✷ ✷

I checked my phone, which I'd left on silent, and saw I had at least a dozen texts from my mom, each one more frenzied than the last.

"Dammit," I said, coming to as if out of a trance. "I completely lost track of time. I have to be home." It was ten at night. I wondered how long it had been since she'd realized I was gone.

"I'll pick you up tomorrow around noon and we'll pay a visit to Dr. Silver."

After this, I knew, there was no way my mom would let me out of her sight.

"No," I said, my phone lighting up with a new influx of irate texts. "That's not a good idea."

"Why not?"

"I have to go, I'm sorry." I stood up and dusted myself off. A call was coming in. "I have to answer this."

"Where the hell are you, Justine?" my mom shrieked, and I winced, giving Ruby a pathetic *I'm sorry* wave. "Do you have any idea how much trouble you're in?"

"Justine, wait," Ruby tried, calling after me. "Don't you want to find out what happened? Justine!"

"I'm coming home," I said into the phone, talking

over her panicked squawking. "Please calm down, I'm coming home." I hung up and sighed deeply. I felt worn out, defeated. I didn't know yet just how defeated I truly was.

✳ ✳ ✳

When I got home, my mom was standing in the alleyway with Detectives Sato and Rayner. Red and white lights swirled from the top of their squad car, projecting a bloody river onto my mom's white stucco garage.

"What's going on?" I asked. It was warm out but I was shivering.

"Justine Childs, you're under arrest," Detective Sato said. "You have the right to remain silent. Anything you say can and will be used against you in a court of law. You have the right to an attorney. If you cannot afford an attorney, one will be provided for you." He put one hand on my shoulder and one on my opposite wrist, then spun me around so he could fasten the handcuffs. It was such a swift and graceful motion, it was almost like dancing.

CHAPTER 8

JUSTINE CHILDS— COLD-BLOODED KILLER?

"I was at the Ace," I insisted for the hundredth time, whimpering and humiliated, "I told you that already."

"Turns out you weren't," Sato said finally, leading me into the station, my wrists bound in handcuffs behind my back. "We checked. They say you didn't get there until five in the morning. According to the autopsy, Miss Kelly died between midnight and 4:00 A.M."

"That doesn't mean I hurt her!" I said. "That's not proof of anything. If I was at the Ace by five, how could I even have time—" I stopped talking as Sato and Rayner pushed me past an open area full of people and into a room with frosted glass walls, then slammed the door shut.

Rayner opened a black ink pad. Sato removed the

handcuffs. My right hand went limp as Sato lifted it, gripping on to my thumb. He plunged my thumb onto the ink pad and rolled it back and forth.

"There's no way you have enough to arrest me," I insisted, fully believing this. "All you know is that I don't have a great alibi. That's it."

"Oh, we got a lot more than that, sweet pea," Sato snickered. "Fingerprints on the athame? Same as the ones on the black coffee you left behind last time you visited us."

"Where's my mom?"

"She's here. You can see her after we book you."

This isn't happening, I told myself, feeling my whole body stiffen and chill. Growing up we had rabbits, thirteen total, my favorite one a rusty strawberry color. I named her Strawberry, the way kids do. One day she got out of her hutch and Princess Leia chased her across the yard, scaring her to death. She didn't mean to hurt her. Strawberry didn't have a single scratch on her. She was untouched. On the outside, at least. On the inside her heart had burst open in one sudden moment. When I found her body it was rigid and ice cold. Literally frozen to death, frozen with fear. Even through her dense coat of fur, she felt icy against my fingers. I wondered if I felt that way now to Sato and Rayner when they touched me. I wondered if a human could be scared to death the way a rabbit could be.

Sato lifted my thumb from the pad and pressed it onto a ripe white sheet of card stock and rolled it again, left and right, like he had moments before in the ink. The swirled grooves of my skin showed up jet black and broken on the page, looking like an alien language, something the extraterrestrials left behind with their pyramids and their moonstones. I squinted sideways on the off chance I could catch a hidden message.

Ask for a lawyer. The thought shot through my mind like a ribbon, slick and shredded.

"I want a lawyer," I said. Sato laughed.

"Of course you do," he said. "If I killed my best friend I'd want a lawyer too."

"I didn't—" I started, but stopped, hearing my dad's voice in my head: *If you're ever arrested, don't say a single word. Innocent or guilty, do not say a single word. Not a single word, do you hear me?* Angry, as if I'd already disobeyed. He'd even make me practice sometimes.

"Justine, you're under arrest," he'd say, sitting casually across from me at the dinner table, inserting some arbitrary reason for my arrest—vandalism, theft, arson. "You have the right to remain silent. Anything you say can and will be used against you in a court of law."

I'd stare, blinking silently back at him, and he'd smile approvingly.

"Can you tell us what you were doing between eight and nine this morning?" He'd readopt his bad-cop persona, my mom looking on, unamused.

I'd keep staring straight ahead, staying quiet.

"Not talking, huh? You know, we have an eyewitness who says they saw you spray painting the side of the science building." Sometimes I wondered where he grabbed these scenarios from, all of them nerdy and slipshod, impossible to take seriously.

I'd shrug, but not say a word.

"Who do you think you're fooling? We have a witness who saw you do it. If you just admit to what you did, we'll let the prosecution know you cooperated and they might go easier on you. But if you keep lying, well, then I won't be able to help you."

Shrug. Smile silently.

"If you were really innocent you'd just tell us where you were between eight and nine. Not telling us makes you look pretty guilty, Justine."

This was where I'd normally break. If I could easily exonerate myself with an alibi, shouldn't I say something and end the suffering then and there? No, not according to my dad. Getting you to try to help yourself was how they'd get you in the end, use every word against you as soon as they had the chance. He told me over and over again how the cops can make even the most innocent person guilty, but only if you talk. Once you're arrested, innocent or guilty, the only power you have is your silence.

These mock interrogations started around age seven, but they picked up in frequency and thoroughness when I got home from Bellflower. That's when he got protective of me, even a little overprotective, after seeing what could happen to me, I guess. That lasted about a year.

Sato guided me by the shoulders against a horizontally striped wall, each line marking an inch of height. In my kitten heels I came up almost to the 5'5" line. *Taylor Swift is five whole inches taller than that,* I caught myself thinking, feeling small and inconsequential.

"Look at the camera," Rayner said, though I couldn't tell where exactly that was. FLASH! It was an unjust burst of light, catching me at my lowest moment with no do-overs. One tear escaped and slid down my cheek. I tried to comfort myself by summoning an image of handsome-as-hell Frank Sinatra in his famous black-and-white mug shot—*see, it's not so bad, it could happen to the best of us!*—but it was no comfort. All I could think was, what had he done to get arrested? And why had I never wondered about that before? Who had he hurt and why had we made it all so glamorous? Then all I could think was how the image had become so ubiquitous that you could even buy it at Target now, and that Frank was probably rolling over in his grave at the thought. *If you're lucky,* I told myself, *one day they'll sell your mug shot in Target too.*

"You have one phone call." Sato introduced me to a mustard-yellow receiver, nodding at it, thumbs tucked into his belt loops. It was heavier than I expected it would be, and so cold pressed up against my ear. I dialed self-consciously, Sato's eyes making it all feel like a performance, like a roundoff double back-flip I had to land just right. My nerves jitterbugged as the low electronic trill went on in loops. Rrrrrrrr. Rrrrrrrrr. Rrrrrrrr. Finally, someone picked up.

"This is Elliot," he said.

"Dad," I croaked wearily, "I need a lawyer."

✳ ✳ ✳

Hours later I was still alone and without answers. I didn't believe they'd really lock me up like that, but next thing I knew I was behind bars. Afraid, breathing shallowly. Wasn't I so obviously innocent? Couldn't they see that in my face?

It wasn't very cold, but my molars chattered violently. My fingertips went lavender. I sat cross-legged with my back against the wall and buried my face in my palms to avoid looking at cell bars the color of chewed mint gum. Adrenaline ran so resolutely through my veins I couldn't worry past the current moment, trapped in the dull, deep present, inescapable like a muddy ocean. I thought about killing myself, the idea floating down from above and anchoring itself into the sandy floor of my mind. I could slice my wrists and not have to think for one more second about Eva-Kate or lawyers or what people were probably out there saying about me. *Athame.* I conjured an image of the shiny blade. Had it really been that sharp? Sharp enough to kill? I hadn't thought so. I had underestimated, miscalculated.

But no, I wouldn't kill myself, I wouldn't even bother trying. The path ahead of me looked grim, but I was morbidly curious to see how it would all unfold. And besides, the free-fall of dread that came with the thought of no longer existing dwarfed any pain of being alive. I'd have to stick around and face the burden of proving my innocence.

At the sound of footsteps, I lifted my head. A man was striding down the hallway, making a somewhat crooked, albeit urgent, beeline for my cell, Detective Sato trailing close behind him. He was tall and looked skinny enough to slip right through the bars of my cell, and as he neared I saw that he wore jeans and a leather jacket, reddish hair slicked carelessly back off his freckled forehead.

"You haven't said anything, have you?" he asked, gripping one of the bars. He was clean-shaven and his face bore no signs of age. He looked like someone who'd hang out with Rob, the kind of kid you'd see plastered all over I Know What You Did Last Night.

"Me?" I asked. There was no one else he could have been talking to.

"Yes, you. Have you said anything to them?"

"Uh . . . no, I mean, I don't think so."

"Can we get this open?" he barked at Sato. "Come on, let's go."

Sato nodded to the guard, who unlocked my cell, then got out of the way.

"What's going on?" I asked, looking back and forth between Sato and this new man. "Who are you?"

"I'm Jack Willoughby. Your new lawyer."

"*You're* my lawyer?" He had long legs and I had to walk fast to keep up with him, like a teacup dog struggling alongside its owner. He was whisking me away down a long, drafty hallway. "How old are you?"

"How is that relevant?" The smell of coffee, cigarettes, and sharply sweet cologne wafted off him as we walked.

"You look, like . . . twenty. Are you old enough to defend me? Are you *good enough* to defend me?" I didn't have the time or wherewithal to be polite. Whenever I was frightened, niceties were the first thing to go out the window, along with any concern about making a good impression.

"I'm twenty-seven," he informed me. "And to be frank, I'm the best that there is."

That shut me up. His confidence was unlike anything I'd ever seen. He wasn't just saying he was the best, he *knew* he was the best. I could see it in his eyes, and it stopped me in my tracks. What was that like, living with the knowledge that you are the best at something? Does it make you happy? Proud? Serene? Or do you take it for granted, like air, and go on being dissatisfied, still having to prove yourself every time someone new enters the room?

"You're going home to await a trial date. In the meantime, do not talk to anybody about the case, do not leave your home. Do you understand? Your parents are outside waiting for you, and for God's sake try to obey them."

He didn't pause after *do you understand*, so I couldn't tell him no, I didn't understand.

"But . . . I didn't do this."

"That's what we'll prove in court."

"Are you sure?"

"Look, I've been out of law school for three years and I haven't lost a case yet."

"Do you believe I'm innocent?"

"That . . . that doesn't matter, Justine," he said, quicker than I was expecting. "Just go home and try to get some rest."

"How could I possibly *rest*? What if we can't prove I'm innocent? If I have to wait around doing nothing I'll lose my mind. Isn't there something I can do?"

"No. That's my job, not yours."

"But . . . But I—"

"Your parents are waiting. Come on, let's get you home." He put one hand on my back and used the other to push open the door.

Stepping outside, I was hit with a tidal wave of light, biting at me, crashing over me in painful blasts. At first I didn't understand. I had lost track of time, but even so, it had to be the middle of the night—the brightness didn't make sense. Then I realized: It wasn't the sun that was blinding me, but a sea of flashbulbs. There were at least a hundred people clamoring to take my picture. Then the chorus came:

Justine, who killed Eva-Kate? FLASH! Justine, did you do it? FLASH! Justine, why'd you do it? FLASH! Justine, where were you two nights ago? Justine, Justine, over here! FLASH! Justine, who do you think did this? FLASH! Justine, is it true you were dating Eva-Kate at the time of her death? FLASH! Justine, do you think you'll go to jail? FLASH! Justine, are you scared? FLASH! Justine, give us a quote! FLASH! Justine, was it self-defense? FLASH! Justine, did anybody have a grudge against Eva-Kate? FLASH! Justine, was it Rob? FLASH! Justine, over here! Over here, Justine! FLASH!

Justine, how much was your bail? FLASH! Justine, who bailed you out? FLASH! Justine, where are you going now? FLASH! Justine, how do you feel? FLASH! FLASH! FLASH! FLASH! JUSTINE! JUSTINE! JUSTINE! JUSTINE! JUSTINE! JUSTINE! JUSTINE! JUSTINE! JUSTINE! JUSTINE!

A pair of guards appeared to part the crowd, and Jack Willoughby handed me off to my parents, who ushered me through the aggravating patchwork of noise and light.

"Take her to my office tomorrow at two thirty," Jack told my parents, handing them a card. "We'll start discussing a plan. It's going to work out; let's stay calm, okay?"

It was hard to believe that all of that commotion was just for me, but when I let myself acknowledge that I was, at least for now, the center of attention, a luminous warmth rolled through my muscles and for a moment, just for one fleeting moment, I had to try not to smile.

✳ ✳ ✳

"This is a goddamn nightmare." My mom put a hand over her heart and took a deep breath. Hot flashes of light hit the car windows like tiny kamikaze assailants.

"Nancy." My dad fidgeted with his twisted seat belt

in the passenger seat, then gave up and left it unbuckled. "She's going to be fine. Jack is an excellent attorney. He'll get the charges dropped before it even goes to trial."

"How do you know that?" my mom quizzed, driving away slowly, trying not to hit any of the dozen paparazzi swarming the car. "He's just a baby, Elliot. Don't you know any *adult* lawyers?"

"It doesn't get better than Jack Willoughby," he said. "Age is just a number."

"Of course," my mom said, the spirit of an eye roll trapped in her words. "How convenient."

"What's that supposed to mean, exactly?"

"Saying 'age is just a number' is the perfect way to justify spending time with people way too young for you." She managed to get past the crowd and let her foot rest heavy on the gas, shooting us past the station and onto Third Street, where two men were playing tug-of-war with a shopping cart.

"Chantal is *very* mature for her age," my dad argued. "It's not like I'm dating a thirty-year-old."

"It's not *like* you're dating a thirty-year-old," my mom clapped back. "But you *are*."

"You wanna talk about age?" My dad smacked the dashboard and I flinched. "Maybe you need to be reminded that you've been screwing a bona fide senior citizen for the past decade."

"Oh, screw you, Elliot." We swerved onto the 110 freeway with a worrisome screech. "How dare you talk like that in front of our daughter."

"I'm confused." He cupped a hand theatrically around his ear. "Am I . . . am I deaf? Or did you attack me first *in front of our daughter*? Who, by the way, Nancy, is being charged with murder, so, you know, isn't exactly a princess herself, is she?"

"*She didn't do it!*" my mother shouted. "Our daughter is not a killer."

"Of course she's not," he sighed, taking the hysteria down a notch. "This is ridiculous. I'm sorry, Justine." He turned around to squeeze my knee. "Everything's going to be okay."

I ignored him, not to prove a point or anything intentional like that, but just because I had too much on my mind to really register either one of them. Their quarreling had become white noise, brushing past me like static in the air.

We dropped my dad off at his new place in North Hollywood, and maybe if I hadn't just been arrested for allegedly murdering the only person I'd ever really loved, I might feel sad that he didn't live with us anymore. But I didn't care. He slammed the door without thanking my mom for the ride, and I didn't care about that either. I put my head against the window and wondered, again, if Jack believed that I was innocent. Did he genuinely not want to know one way or the other? I needed him to believe me. I cared more about if he thought I was innocent than he seemed to care if I was or wasn't. I closed my eyes and, within seconds, I was asleep.

CHAPTER 9

JUSTINE CHILDS BUILDS A CASE

*A*s she'd been instructed, my mom took me to see Jack Willoughby the following day at two thirty. The offices of Thatcher, Chance, and Shaw were classic and pared down. A little stuffy. Some carpet, lots of marble. Or maybe it was marble laminate. Various degrees from prestigious schools hanging from wood-paneled walls. We sat across from Jack, who rolled his sleeves up and greeted us with a warm smile.

"Thank you for taking the time to make it over today," he said. "I'm looking forward to getting down to work."

"Well, it's not like we had a choice," I grumbled. I wasn't trying to be rude; I was just so anxious I couldn't keep it down. My heart pounded. I felt as though my skeleton were trying to jump out of my skin and dash away.

"*Justine*," my mom scolded, "Come on."

"I'm sorry," I said, meaning it.

"I get it," he assured me. "This is extremely stressful. But you're in good hands, and the strategy here is simple."

"Excellent," my mom said, sitting up stick straight. "Let's talk strategy."

"First off, there'll be a fitness hearing. That will determine whether or not Justine is unfit for juvenile court. If she's found to be unfit, she'll be tried as an adult."

"She's absolutely fit for juvenile court," my mom said. "She's only sixteen."

"It's . . . possible, yes, but—"

"What would the difference be?" I asked.

"In juvenile court, the verdict is decided by a judge, no jury, and you can't be sentenced to jail, only juvenile hall. In adult court, you have a jury to decide on a verdict, and, of course, you can be sentenced to jail for any number of years."

"Jesus Christ." My chest tightened. My mom slipped herself a Xanax and rubbed her temples.

"What are the factors that would determine where she's tried?" she asked.

"Past records, the nature of the crime . . . but let's put that out of our minds," Jack said, seeing the distress he'd caused, and made a swooping gesture with his hands as if wiping the information off a screen. "Let's proceed now as if you'll be standing trial in juvenile court. The way I see it, there's not enough evidence to prove your guilt. We have one eyewitness, who I can prove unreliable, and besides that, it's just the fingerprints on the murder weapon."

"That second one is a pretty big deal," I pointed out. "Isn't it?"

"Not necessarily," he said. "Just because your prints were found on the knife doesn't mean they were from that night. And besides, there were other prints too. Yours weren't the only ones."

"Who else's prints were found?" my mom asked.

"I don't know." He glanced at his notes. "They don't know yet."

"I bet anything they're Olivia's," I said.

"Who's Olivia?" he asked. "And what makes you think that?"

"She was a friend of Eva-Kate's. She never really liked me. But I saw her last night and she said something . . . Well, okay, so, I asked her a question and she said, 'As if I would tell you, ya psycho bitch.'"

"And?" my mom asked.

"Go on," Jack encouraged me.

"And the thing is, I realized I'd seen on Eva-Kate's Instagram someone had written, 'I hope you die, *ya*

Barbie.' So, I mean, that has to point to something, right? Not everyone talks like that, you know? It's kind of specific."

"Maybe." Jack wrote it down. "It's not really enough to cause reasonable doubt, but it might be worth looking into. Do you know where she was the night of Eva-Kate's death? Or why she might want to hurt her?"

"She was there, at Eva-Kate's house," I said. "But a motive? I don't know."

"Okay, well, for now you don't need to worry about that. For now all you need to do is stay out of trouble and under the radar. Forget about what other people did or didn't do, and let's stay focused on the fact that the prosecution's evidence is weak and I'll be able to take it apart in court. Does that make sense?"

Hardly, I thought. "Sure," I said, forcing a smile. But no way was I going to go home and rest easy knowing I was the main suspect in the death of a national star.

✷ ✷ ✷

When I woke up, blackout curtains had been installed on my windows and everything was dark. I had to peer between a slit in the fabric to orient myself. An overeager sunbeam sliced into the room and I jerked back, startled. The sound of claws against wood told me Princess Leia was somewhere in the room, blessed with having no idea of what was happening in my life. The truth was

I could go to jail and she'd be fine. At that thought, I reached for the half-empty bottle of scotch stored under my bed and took a big gulp, the liquid flaring down my throat in soothing strands.

With the edge taken slightly off, I reached for my phone and unlocked it. In my experience—and maybe you can relate to this—Instagram is a colorfully curated escape from the doldrums of real life, an easy way to check out, then check back in whenever you feel ready. But not today. Not this time. I opened the app and was met with torrential notifications. Likes and tags, follow requests and comments. I scrolled and scrolled, seeing no end to any of it. Thousands of comments, then hundreds of thousands, the numbers racing up faster than I could blink. My heart pumped, eyelids flickered. If the numbers themselves were the high, the comments were the comedown.

You are a psycho murderer, one read. *Too bad California doesn't have the death penalty,* said another. I should have stopped there, but Lord knows I've never had that level of willpower.

> Justine Childs is a cold-blooded killer.
> I hope you rot in hell, you social-climbing whore.
> You're not fooling anyone, devil's child!
> If Eva-Kate never met you she'd still be alive.
> Kill yourself.
> God is judging you.

Whore.

Kill yourself.

Are you happy now, bitch?

How do you sleep at night?

Kill yourself.

Psychopath.

This is what evil looks like.

Of course she's guilty, she was jealous of Eva-Kate and couldn't handle it!

You think you're gonna get away with this but you're not!

Kill yourself.

Cold-hearted bitch!

Morally FUCKED.

How can you stand yourself?

You disgust me.

Kill yourself.

You'll get what you deserve.

You're not even pretty, LOL!

This skank killed Eva-Kate!

Die, die, die.

Kill yourself.

Bitch.

Psycho killer.

Kill yourself.

Whore.

Tramp.

Kill yourself.

Kill yourself.

Kill yourself.

Kill yourself.

Each one felt like a punch to the stomach. It didn't matter if I was innocent; the world was going to skewer me for this. But then, through the dense overlay of tears, I caught a glimpse of solace.

Y'all got it twisted. Justine is 100% innocent. Link in bio.

The comment was written by someone going by @Kenzie.Malone. Her account was mostly flowers and seascapes, all of it adhering to a strict pink-and-blue color scheme. Of the one hundred and twelve photos posted, she wasn't in any of them. The link in her bio read: FreeQueenJustine.com. I clicked, exhilarated.

The link took me to a bare-bones website with my name and face plastered at the top. Underneath my face a titled typewriter font read: I.N.N.O.C.E.N.T. And beneath that:

Hey, guys, my name is Kenzie Malone, and I believe very strongly that Justine Childs did not kill Eva-Kate Kelly. I intend to do everything in my power to prove her innocence, and I hope you'll join me in this mission. If you're not convinced, here are the reasons I personally believe she couldn't have committed this heinous crime:

1. No motive—why on earth would Justine kill her best friend? As far as we know, there was no conflict between the two.

2. Unlike Justine, plenty of people out there had a problem with Eva-Kate (to protect myself, I can't post any theories publicly, but my DMs are open if you wish to discuss).

3. She wasn't at the house at the time of the murder.

4. She has no history of being a violent person.

If you'd like to donate money to the Justine Childs Innocence Project, click HERE. If you're a true Eva-Kate Kelly fan, you'll want to know the truth about what happened to her, so I suggest you stop wasting your time by barking up the wrong tree. Let's find the real killer!

Yours truly,

Kenzie

Beneath her message, a carpet of comments unfolded, these ones taking on a completely different tone than the ones posted to my Instagram:

> Justine is an angel, she couldn't hurt a fly!
>
> Too pretty to be a killer, smh.
>
> Donated!
>
> INNOCENT!
>
> Honestly, why would such a quality human being waste her time with trash like Eva-Kate anyway?
>
> She WILL be exonerated.
>
> LEAVE JUSTINE ALONE (to the tune of Leave Britney Alone, LOL).
>
> Justine, if you're reading this, we got your back!
>
> It was Rob.
>
> Donated!
>
> Look at that baby face! She's too cute!
>
> Leave her alone, damn.
>
> Eva-Kate was friends with shady-ass people, Justine is not one of them!
>
> Donated!
>
> Let me know how I can help.
>
> I bet it was Rob.
>
> If you think that girl could kill anyone you are TRIPPING.
>
> Her mom was after her money.
>
> Aren't the cops looking into Rob? It's always the boyfriend.

Innocent.

SO innocent.

Rob. It was Rob. Haven't you seen Law and Order?

It's always the boyfriend!!

Free Justine!

Justine is Queen.

Bae.

Donated!

WE LOVE YOU JUSTINE!

Justine is an ANGEL.

It had to be Rob. I mean, come on.

Thanks for making this site, let's get her in the clear!

OMG she is SO innocent.

Leave Justine Alone is the new Leave Britney Alone.

#freeJustine

They went on and on. I read to the bottom and closed my eyes. How odd, I thought, how little any of these people knew about me, about who I am and about what actually happened. But they had such big, certain opinions anyway. I couldn't remember the last time I was certain about anything, let alone the life of a total stranger. They thought they knew me and I felt sad for them. *So this is what it's like*, I thought, *when massive amounts of strangers think they know you.* Dizzy and disoriented, soaring and shaky like the ground has been pulled out from beneath you. It was a thrill and a horror. The strange comfort of a fever. I didn't know if I liked it. I didn't hate it.

Kenzie Malone had set up a corner of the site for "Anonymous Theories," but after thirty minutes of scrolling, I saw nothing even remotely useful. All of it boiled down to: It was Rob. It was Rob. It was Rob. *Can't one of you help me?* I thought, pleading then with the universe, *Can't somebody help me?* Jack Willoughby would. Maybe. I prayed.

I typed his name into the search bar and traded FreeQueenJustine.com for nine Google search results. I clicked on the first one, an article on CHOMPER.com. "Prodigy Jack Willoughby Makes Legal History as Youngest Lawyer to Acquit Defendant in Murder Trial." The article read: *After almost one year in court, Jessica and Rebecca Bianchi walk free. Accused of slaying their parents in cold blood, the twenty-two-year-old twins were found not guilty.*

"No, I don't think they did it," said juror Althea Judkins. "Of course, it's possible, there was some evidence that said maybe so, but on the other hand there was overwhelming evidence that a third party was in the house that night. So, you know. Reasonable doubt and whatnot."

"Yes, I'm extremely happy with the outcome," said Willoughby. "But I'm not at all surprised. Once Jessica

told me she heard a voice that night, a voice that wasn't her sister's, I knew we could prove somebody else was in that house. It was simple: My clients were innocent. I knew that from the beginning, and now the jury has spoken."

What about me, Jack? I stopped to think. Am I innocent? Then I kept reading: At only twenty-four years old, defense attorney Jack Willoughby makes legal history as the youngest lawyer to ever win a murder trial. After credibly establishing the possibility of the presence of a third person in the Bianchi house the night of the killings, Willoughby convinced the jury to acquit. Authorities are now investigating Lawrence Shaeffer, boyfriend of Rebecca Bianchi, whose footprints were found in the home and whose fingerprints were found on the shotguns used to kill Mr. and Mrs. Bianchi.

The article went on for a little while after that, but I had all the information I needed. And I needed to talk to Dr. Silver. If somehow I could prove he'd come by that night, maybe they'd check the athame again and find his fingerprints, and then just maybe . . . maybe everything would be okay again and I could go on to live some semblance of a normal life, find inner peace, or something like it. Doubtful. The word flared up in fiery neon branded somewhere in the back of my mind.

I opened Instagram to message Ruby and saw that my following had gone up to one hundred and eighty thousand. One hundred eighty thousand people. Following *me.* It was a rush of champagne bubbles to the head. *Champagne,* I thought. If a hundred and eighty thousand followers isn't something to celebrate, then what is? I made sure my mom wasn't around, then popped a bottle from my dad's cabinet and poured the overeager liquid into a glass flute. I brought the glass to my lips, then tilted my head back so the champagne slid swiftly down my throat, sparkling all the way down. Satisfied with the instant buzz, I returned to my room.

I found Ruby on Instagram (@Ruby2sday, 43.8K followers) and DMed her: *Ready to see the Dr. now. ASAP.*

She wrote back almost immediately: *be ready in an hour.*

So I was.

If I went out the back into the alley, I'd risk my mom seeing me through her office curtains, so I went out the front and power walked, baseball cap pulled over my eyes, glancing over my shoulder every few steps, to the end of the street, where Ruby idled in a vintage Mustang. Dusty sunset pink, top down.

"I made an appointment at his Beverly Hills office under a fake name," she said with a coyote-sly smile. "We'll pretend like we're there for a consultation, then get him to admit what he did. I'll record it on my phone."

"How were you able to get us in so last minute?"

"This guy's reputation has kind of sucked for a while, he's just rebuilding."

"Okay, but . . ." She was so excited, I didn't want to rain down hard on her parade, so I treaded lightly. "I'm not sure that . . . I mean, do you think he's really just going to admit to murder just like that?"

"Not to *murder*," she explained. "Just to being at the house that night. That's all we need."

This felt more realistic, more doable, and I relaxed a little.

"Do you mind putting the top up?" I asked. "I really shouldn't be out."

CHAPTER 10

JUSTINE CHILDS VISITS PLASTIC SURGEON

The offices of Dr. David K. Silver were located twelve floors above a Bank of America and had tall, tinted glass windows overlooking Santa Monica Boulevard, which looked distant and flat from that distance, the cars like kindergarten toys. Ruby, with her hair tied back and face half hidden behind black Balenciaga cat-eyes, scribbled furiously on a stack of intake papers using the name Jordan Hayes, while I accidentally found myself in a staring contest with a fat clown fish squirming inside an aquarium that protruded from the wall like a pregnant belly. I was either too tired or too nervous to look away. The slick, sick feeling in the pit of my stomach was as if I'd swallowed that clown fish whole. I twisted my hair up into my baseball cap and put on my reading glasses, hoping this would be enough for me to go relatively undetected. If Dr. Silver recognized me—or Ruby, for that matter—we wouldn't get a word out of him. And I needed that word.

A nurse with freshly bleached hair and too much lip liner called Jordan Hayes. Ruby explained to her in a suddenly British accent that I was her sister.

"If it's all right with you, I absolutely *need* to bring her into the consultation," she explained. "She's the voice of reason in my life and without her I'd make the *stupidest* decisions. She's here to make sure I don't leave here today with an entirely new face."

"Sure, mhm," the nurse said blandly with a routine smile, apparently impervious to Jordan's awkwardly foreign charm. I, on the other hand, was very amused and had to look down at the white linoleum floor to keep from laughing. The nurse directed us down the hall and soon we were alone in a heavily air-conditioned, pine-scented room with a Hawaiian seascape rippling on a flat-screen TV to the melodic tune of a pan flute. Floor-to-ceiling mirrors flanked the TV. I looked up and saw that the ceiling itself was a mirror. The bird's-eye view of myself in that black baseball hat made me feel like a pawn in a game of chess.

"Let me do the talking, yeah?" Ruby said. "You're not the smoothest with words. And your nerves are *palpable* right now. No offense."

"None taken," I said, though I was, of course, offended. But I was even more grateful for the permission to stay silent.

"There's something kinda calming about this place," she said, hopping up onto the reclining chair covered in waxy paper. "It's good to know there's somewhere to go when I decide to get rid of the crow's-feet I can already see starting to form on my face."

I didn't think Ruby had crow's-feet, and I told her as much.

"You know what, Justine?" she said. "Thank you."

She wore palazzo pants striped with blue, pink, and white, and a mustard-yellow front-tie crop top. I'd have loved to be able to pull something like that off, but how could I when even the briefest of lingering gazes turned me into an uncomfortable, shameful, stiffened, insecure, frigid, self-loathing stone? I was deep into my sixteenth year of craving attention and finding that I couldn't handle even a little bit of it.

There was a quick knock at the door and Dr. Silver strode in. "Hello, hello!" he announced himself, kicking the door shut with the polished toe of his shoe and holding out one big, almost oversized, hand to Ruby. "I'm Dr. Silver, pleased to meet you." He grinned ear to ear, dimples pushed out to the far sides of his face. I was stunned by how good-looking he was. I'd been expecting some old and ugly creep, a blatant and professional predator. But although he was older, I guessed somewhere in his sixties, he was easily the most handsome man I'd ever seen. And maybe he'd only said nine words to us, but so far there was nothing creepy about him.

"I'm Jordan." Ruby readopted her British accent and gestured to me. "This is my sister, Rosalind."

"Hi, Rosalind." He held my hand in both of his and gripped it gently. His eyes were radiant, sizzling green and bookended by fine, friendly crinkles. They looked directly into mine and idled there for a moment. My heart thumped and I prayed he wouldn't know who I was.

"How can I help you today?" He sat down on a leather stool and looked from me to Ruby, then back to me again. It occurred to me that he looked more than a little like Dennis Quaid, and I wondered if his cheekbones and jawline were naturally so sculpted, or if he'd had them done. This was the world of plastic surgery, after all, a world where you could cut and sculpt yourself to perfection, and then far past the point of perfection into the surreal, and then into the grotesque.

"Oh, it's just me," Ruby explained. "Rosalind's only here for moral support."

"Okay then." He rolled up his starchy white sleeves and I noted the impeccable alignment of his teeth. "What improvements are you looking to make for yourself?"

"Where do I even begin?" she laughed.

"You tell me, gorgeous." He snapped on a pair of latex gloves and moved to get a closer look at her. "Though I can't imagine what you're unhappy with. I mean, look at this bone structure."

"Oh, thank you." Ruby pretended to be very flattered by this wooden compliment, or maybe she really *was* flattered; I hadn't known her long enough to tell. "But it's really just my lips. I can't stand how thin they are."

"Ah, well." He tilted his head from side to side, appraising her mouth. "Your lips are perfectly fine, but of course I can help if you'd like to add a little extra volume. No harm in that."

"See?" Ruby stuck out her chin to me, triumphantly, as if I'd told her otherwise. "A little collagen injection never hurt anyone." She turned to Dr. Silver. "Rosalind's been telling me if I get my lips done I'll look trashy, or like a duck, but I don't see why that would be the case. I mean, lip injections never looked trashy on Eva-Kate Kelly, so why should they look trashy on me?"

I flinched at her name. I braced myself for his reaction. His jaw clenched. A vein pulsed from his temple.

"She had beautiful lips," he said, his smile faltering, deflating at the corners.

"I hope I don't sound disrespectful." Ruby was batting her eyelashes. "But do you think they were, you know, fake?"

"I don't like that word." He forced his smile back into place. "I prefer enhanced. And yes, hers were. Eva-Kate was a client of mine."

"Oh." Ruby pretended to be surprised. "I'm so sorry for your loss."

I was surprised he'd been so willing to admit it. She had just been murdered; shouldn't he be playing his cards so much closer to his chest? Shouldn't he pretend he didn't know her? I would, if I were him.

"Thank you, that's all right." He clapped his hands together and held them there. "Now, should we get down to business?"

"God, I mean, it's just so sad," Ruby went on, pretending not to hear him. "Someone dying so young. Do you have any idea what happened to her?"

"Um . . ." He stalled for a second. "No, we weren't close. I don't know anything about what happened."

"You sure?" Ruby pressed. "I mean, if you knew her, maybe you knew who might have wanted to—"

"Like I said," he interrupted, "we weren't close. Believe me, I wish I knew what happened. It's awful knowing someone is out there who cut her life short. Nobody deserves to die so young, and so violently. But I don't think now is the time to discuss—"

"When was the last time you saw her?" There was an almost chipper bounce in Ruby's voice.

"I don't know." He grew stern. "But I'm not talking

about this now. I'm happy to continue the consultation but I'm afraid I won't be discussing Eva-Kate Kelly any further."

"You know," Ruby said, reassuming her American accent, "we have somebody who says they saw you come by her house the night she died."

"*Excuse me?*" He crossed his arms, recoiling like he'd been slapped. "Who would say that? That's absurd."

"Is it?" Ruby raised an eyebrow.

"Yes. It is. And who are you? Who are you to come in here and start accusing me like this? You should leave." He pulled the door open and jerked his head into the open space. "*Now.*"

Ruby didn't move.

"We should," I told her, standing up. "We should leave. Let's go." I had stood up too quickly. The baseball cap toppled off my head, letting my hair cascade in tangled, chaotic waves.

Dr. Silver squinted at me. Then his eyes widened in recognition. "You're the girl who killed her," he said. "You're all over the tabloids!"

"I did *not* kill her," I said, the word *kill* coming out choked and broken. "I wasn't even there when she died. But you were. London Miller saw you. And I'm sure the security footage will confirm it."

He shut the door. "London saw me?" he asked. His

voice was calm, though his body tensed like a jungle animal's. "She said that?"

"Yep." Ruby smirked. "So, is it true?"

"I may have been there." He put his hands up as if to say *don't shoot*. "But I didn't hurt her. I came by, yes, but she wasn't there. She texted me, said to come over, so I did. But nobody came to the door, and she wouldn't answer her phone. I guess I was too late. I would never hurt her. I . . . you don't understand . . . I love her."

"That's disgusting," I said. "She was only sixteen."

"Oh, *come on*." He rolled his eyes. "You knew her. She wasn't exactly your average sixteen-year-old."

I couldn't argue with him there; I had often felt the same way about her.

"And you didn't care that when kids and teenagers seem older than they are it's because of some horrible trauma?" asked Ruby.

"I didn't . . . that hasn't been proven, has it?"

"It doesn't matter," Ruby said. "The point is, she may have not been *like* a sixteen-year-old, but she *was* sixteen," said Ruby. "So it's still statutory rape."

"Whoa, whoa," he said, stepping back. "Who said anything about—I mean, we never . . . I never tried anything like that with her. Sure, she flirted, and yeah, I had feelings, but I know the law."

"Okay, so, she texted you that night and said to come over. We'll never know why she did that, or if she really did, but either way you ended up there, hoping something might happen. I mean, right, why else would you go to a young girl's house at night besides hoping you might get some action?"

"That's not—"

"But then when you made a move, she rejected you. Humiliated, you freaked out and things got out of hand. Maybe you didn't mean to kill her."

I flinched. If her theory was true, then what would stop him from taking us both out right then and there?

"Girls, listen to me," he said instead. "I did go over that night, but by the time I arrived, nobody was there. Or at least nobody came to the door. The place was empty."

I had left by then, that was for sure, and maybe so had everyone else. Including whoever killed her. Maybe he really had no idea that Eva-Kate hadn't come to the door because she was floating facedown in the water outside.

"You need to tell the police that you were there," I said. "That she texted you but wasn't there by the time you arrived. That could help them figure out what really happened."

"I don't think so. They'd assume I did it. Right now they think it was you," he said. "If they knew I'd been there, who do you think they'd pin the whole thing on? The tiny manic pixie whatever girl, or the six-foot-tall man making a late-night house call?"

"So you're going to let me take the fall for something I didn't do?"

"How do I know you didn't?"

"Because I wasn't there. I was at the Ace Hotel."

"If you have an alibi, then why'd they arrest you?"

I curled my lips under my teeth. "Because," I said, "I hadn't technically gotten to the hotel yet. But I was on my way, I swear to God."

"Didn't they find your fingerprints on the weapon?"

"Yes, but . . . I mean . . . how does that prove anything? She let me hold it just a few days earlier!" My breathing was getting shallow. My chest felt dry and tight. "But I didn't do it!" A tear slid down my cheek. "How could I? I'm just a tiny manic pixie whatever girl, you said so yourself. And if you don't come forward about being there that night, I'm going to go to juvy until I'm eighteen. Or if they decide to try me as an adult, I could spend the rest of my life in prison. Do you know what they do to you in there? They do *cavity searches* on a regular basis. I'll get *shanked*. Look at me, jail would end me. So, I mean, did you see *anything* that night? Anything suspicious? Or maybe you can just tell them what you *didn't* see. You didn't see me, right? Can't you tell them that?"

I was full-on crying then. I didn't want to be, but I couldn't stop. I realized the champagne buzz I'd had was gone and wondered if we could stop at the liquor store on our way home. The wall clock read 3:02 P.M., which meant I had a little under an hour before my mom would be finished with her patients and notice I was gone.

"Please don't cry." Dr. Silver pressed his hands into a pathetic prayer position. "We can figure this out. I'm sure we can find some middle ground that would be good enough for both of us. Some way I don't have to confess to being there that night, but you also don't have to be found guilty."

"How?" I asked. "I don't see how that could happen."

"Well." He paused, tapping his nose with one still-gloved finger. "What if I told you who I think did it? What if somehow I could drum up the proof you need?"

"You mean . . . you don't think I did it?"

"Not really. No. I don't know, you just don't give off killer vibes. You definitely don't *look* like one. What do you weigh, like ninety pounds?"

"I'm not telling you my weight." I wiped the tears from my eyes. "But you're right. I couldn't have done what they said I did."

"I don't know if you could, but I don't think you did. Mostly because you don't have a motive, and I know somebody who did."

"Who?" Ruby perked up. "Tell us."

"The girl's sister."

"*Liza?*" Ruby blinked. "Are you fucking kidding me?"

"Nope. Not kidding. She and Eva-Kate never had a good relationship."

"Understatement," said Ruby. "But that was nothing

new. And she didn't hate Eva-Kate enough to kill her. I saw her at the funeral. She was destroyed about it."

"Are you sure about that? Eva-Kate's not the only talented actress in that family."

"You think she was pretending to be sad? Why would she want Eva-Kate dead?"

"The top three reasons people commit murder are revenge, jealousy, and greed," he proclaimed. "I'd say for Liza it was a little of each."

Liza had told me that when the show decided they only needed one twin playing Jennie, they offered it to Liza first, but she had turned it down because she knew how badly Eva-Kate wanted it. But what if that had been a lie? What if they had given it to Eva-Kate and fired Liza? What if Liza had resented Eva-Kate this whole time, watching her sister rise to stardom while she faded away in the San Fernando Valley? What if she hated her for it? What if, all along, it had been Liza who hated Eva-Kate, quietly plotting revenge under the radar?

✳ ✳ ✳

"I have to go home," I said as Ruby took us west on Santa Monica and onto the 405 North. "Where are you going?"

"You can't go home yet! We have to talk to Liza."

"Oh, no, no, no," I begged. "That is a bad idea, Ruby."

"You still want to get to the bottom of this, don't you? You still against going to jail?"

"Yes, but . . ."

"Then we need to talk to her. Immediately. Same plan as before: I'll do the talking and record everything on my phone. You don't have to say a word. And also, you don't have a choice. Unless you want to roll out of my car onto the 405, you're coming with me."

✳ ✳ ✳

I trailed behind her as she marched up to the McKelvoy front door. I chewed methodically at the inside of my lip, breaking off tiny pieces of skin from the bottom left corner until blood broke through.

"Liza?" Ruby called, pounding on the door with the heel of her palm. "Liza? It's Ruby. I need to talk to you."

The curtains were drawn but I peered through the middle slit and saw that all the lights were off inside.

"I don't think they're home," I said.

"I bet they are. They just don't wanna talk."

"If they don't want to talk, they don't want to talk. Let's go."

"Not so fast." She brushed me off, then screamed at the top of her lungs, "LIZA MCKELVOY, GET YOUR ASS DOWN HERE. I'M NOT LEAVING UNTIL YOU DO!"

Just then, the door swung open. It was Debbie, freshly platinum haired and spray tanned.

"Stop screaming," she said. "Ruby, what do you want?

And what the hell are *you* doing here?" She pointed at me. "I don't want you on my property."

I took a few steps back, getting ready to run if I had to.

"Debbie, I just need to talk to Liza, it won't take long."

"She's not here," she said, glaring over Ruby's shoulder at me.

"Can you tell me where she is?"

"I actually have no idea. Rob came by last night and in the morning they were gone."

"Rob?" said Ruby. "I thought they broke up?"

"Yeah, well, they're back together now. And God only knows where."

CHAPTER 11

JUSTINE CHILDS—A SEMESTER WITHOUT SCHOOL?

*S*eptember came and the unlucky among us went back to school. It was decided for me that I'd take the semester off, something I'd prayed for more than once in my lifetime. What a dream, I'd always believed, to be that rare thing, the kid who doesn't have to show up for orientation, the kid who's just gone. Finally, it was my turn to be gone, but in being gone from the world, the world was gone from me. I was a Rapunzel of my own making, hidden away with nothing to keep me company but my own ruminations. I chewed on memories like bubble gum: Eva-Kate's laugh ringing out into the air, crisp and metallic and one of a kind. We were supposed to be friends forever. We were supposed to be even more. Where had she gone? And where had it gone wrong?

There was that voice mail from my mom, for one. The athame, for another.

On Instagram I saw Riley and Maddie and Abbie drinking milkshakes at Cafe 50's, laughing hysterically in their gym clothes, riding Bird scooters on the Third Street Promenade. In an alternate universe I was right there with them: a universe where I had never met Eva-Kate, a universe without Cobalts or Crimsons, without Ruby or the Roosevelt or the flashbulbs. I shuddered to think of it, how easily we can take a slight turn that leads us so dramatically away from what would have been. It happens all the time.

On Instagram I saw Riley and Maddie and Abbie spending Thanksgiving with their families, the cranberry-colored decorations and wrinkled relatives, the turkeys in their helplessness looking bloated and obscene. I filled with dread on their behalf, the turkeys, that this was what it had all come down to for them, that they'd lived and died to be a greasy centerpiece of an American lie.

On Instagram I saw London and Olivia letting Thanksgiving pass them by entirely, poolside in bikinis and fur coats drinking champagne out of the bottle, kissing on the lips. Was that just how things were in their world, I wondered, a constant charade of intimacy? Was that what it had been with me and Eva-Kate? Was that all it was? I chased that lurking thought away with whiskey I'd started hiding in a teal-blue Hydro Flask under my bed, and I watched *Donnie Darko* on repeat, because the more times I saw it the closer it came to making sense, and all I really wanted was for things to make sense. I wanted to make sense.

I read and reread a text from Rob that I'd received the day Ruby and I learned he and Liza were gone:

Hi Justine,

I know you know I left town with Liza, and you're probably thinking that it looks shady. I know you're going to be reading way too much into this, so I just wanted to clarify: We didn't leave town because we have anything to hide, we left town because Los Angeles is a sick, sad place. It killed Eva-Kate and it was killing us too. I hope you understand that, and I hope one day you get out too. Rob

And when Ruby came around with wildfire theories about where Rob and Liza were hiding, I'd hear her out, and I'd share my whiskey, even though she never came any closer to tracking them down. I knew with my luck, she never would. And so what if she did—could they have done this? Would people ever believe that?

Then I got a call. "I want you to stay calm." It was Jack's voice on the phone. My mom had handed it to me, saying *your lawyer* with so much contempt, as if it were my fault that I needed a lawyer.

"Then you shouldn't have said that," I answered.

Involuntarily, I started digging my teeth into my bottom lip, my heart fluttering up in my throat like I'd swallowed a bird.

"Your fitness hearing has been scheduled for next week. That will determine if your case can stay in juvenile court."

I'd known this had to happen, but it had snuck up on me anyway like two hands closing around my neck from behind.

"Justine? You okay?"

"I'm calm," I lied.

"Okay . . ." He didn't believe me. "I'm going to need you to come downtown tomorrow for a psych evaluation."

"Why?"

"Understanding your psychological state will help the judge make a decision. And it might help me argue the case for keeping you out of adult court."

"So, what, I have to talk to a therapist?"

"It shouldn't take long," he assured me.

"Are they going to try to figure out if I'm crazy?"

"Your sanity will play a part, sure. But you seem like a stable girl to me. I'm guessing they'll see that too."

They're going to need to know about Bellflower, I thought. Then my image as a "stable girl" would go right out the window.

"Jack," I said. "I don't want to go to jail."

"Of course you don't," he said. "I'm doing everything in my power to make sure that doesn't happen."

I stared into a glass of water on my nightstand until it blurred.

"Justine, are you there?" he asked.

"I'll see you tomorrow," I said, and hung up before he could hear the tears and tightness in my voice. *It's not gonna happen*, I told myself, reaching for the Hydro Flask, *it's not gonna happen.* I pressed PLAY on *Donnie Darko* and Jake Gyllenhaal was saying, "I just hope that when the world comes to an end, I can breathe a sigh of relief, because there will be so much to look forward to." His face, the innocent sleepiness of it, was such a comfort, and for a second everything was okay.

CHAPTER 12

JUSTINE CHILDS EVALUATED BY CLINICAL PSYCHIATRIST

*D*r. Morton was the forensic psychiatrist, and it was up to him to determine my psychological maturity. Did I have the mind of an adult or a child? I myself was eager to know the answer, but suspected it was neither. Dr. Morton wore a slate-gray suit and matching tie. He was youthful with a fresh haircut and looked like he'd just been flown in from some forensic psychiatrist factory where they crank them out on a conveyor belt, one by one.

I felt at ease sliding into the vinyl chair across from him. Therapists were people I understood, and myself was a topic I liked discussing.

"Justine, hi." He smiled and the skin around his eyes crinkled. "I'm Dr. Morton. You can call me Daniel, if you want."

"Okay, Daniel," I said, glancing around the room and noticing a long horizontal mirror embedded into the cinder-block wall. "Are we being watched?"

"No," he said, "but I am recording this."

"Right," I said, keeping an eye on the mirror.

"I'm just going to ask you a few questions and hopefully get to know you a little bit, okay?"

"Yep."

"How old are you, Justine?"

"I'm sixteen."

"You go to school?"

"No . . . I'm taking a break. I have to get ready for the trial."

"But you used to go to school?"

"Of course. I finished tenth grade at Santa Monica High School this past summer. Hopefully if I don't get sent to jail I'll go back next semester."

"So, you liked school, then?"

"Sometimes."

"But . . . sometimes not?"

"I'm terrible at math and science. I did get an A in ninth-grade chemistry, but that's only because I had sixth period free so I sat through every lecture twice."

"Do you have friends at school?"

"I have three best friends. Maddie, Abbie, and Riley. They've been my best friends since . . . I don't even know how long. We met in elementary school."

"So you're pretty tight with them, then."

"You could say that, yes."

"Did they meet Eva-Kate Kelly?"

"Um . . . no."

"Why not?"

"I guess we had started to drift apart."

"Hm, why's that?" He pretended to pout.

Because they wouldn't grow up, I thought, *because they lacked imagination. Because I couldn't confide in them anymore.*

"I don't really want to talk about that," I said. "Next question, please."

"Okay . . . have you ever been involved in any gang activity?"

"What?" I laughed. "No."

"What about a history of drug use?"

"I don't use drugs recreationally, if that's what you mean."

"Are you prescribed anything by a psychiatrist?"

"Prozac for depression, Xanax as needed for anxiety."

"How often would you say you need your anxiety medication?"

All the fucking time, I thought.

"Weekly," I said. "Once a week. Maybe twice."

"What happens if you don't take it?"

"I could end up having a panic attack."

"Can you describe what a panic attack feels like?"

"My heart races and my throat feels like it's closing up. Sometimes I get dizzy. It's pure dread, like the world is ending. If it gets bad enough I'll have to scream into a pillow."

"On a scale from one to ten, how bad was the worst panic attack you ever had?"

✖ ✖ ✖

The worst panic attack I ever had? Well, that would have to be when I was thirteen and my panic got so bad the doctors called it *psychotic*. I'd been alone in my room one night watching *Gossip Girl*, happily enough, when I was suddenly hit by the idea that I should write out my entire life story up to that point. At first it felt like a good idea, then, as I kept writing, it felt like an absolute necessity, like I absolutely had to keep going until it was finished. The drive was intense. I stayed up all night writing frantically, filling a blue composition notebook with stories from my early childhood—catching frogs on East Coast summer vacations, horseback riding lessons with Riley in Topanga Canyon, a brief stint with ballet classes, my *Beauty and the Beast*–themed fourth birthday party—and when the sun rose and I had to go to school, I took the notebook with me and kept writing throughout the entire day.

I stayed up again that night, and the night after that, but the more I wrote the slipperier the words became—they'd pop into my head but slide away before I could get them down on paper—and so I had to write faster. My hand ached and started to cramp, but I kept going.

On the fourth night I paused for a moment and looked out my window. The streetlamps were off and the sky was black as ink. It was so dark I couldn't imagine it ever being light again. That's when the panic set in. Dread like a wall of scalding-hot water crashed over me. I felt in my heart that if I were to close my eyes, even for a second, the sun would never rise again. That would be the beginning of the end of the world as we knew it. The responsibility was astronomical, but I didn't think I had a choice.

I stopped writing, but stayed awake for two more days and nights just trying to keep the sun rising each morning. My parents knew something was wrong—I was staring off into space and slurring my speech—but they didn't say anything. At least not to me. They just watched me a little more closely.

The next night was when my mind really turned on me. That's when the message switched. It told me I'd had it wrong all along: I wasn't the solution, I was the problem, and if I wanted to save the world I'd have to kill myself. But I couldn't kill myself; I was too afraid to die. So instead I wrote about it, about the guilt I felt over being too afraid to do what had to be done to save the world. About how I couldn't think of a way to die that didn't terrify me.

My mom found the notebook. She packed my suitcase and drove me to Bellflower.

Bellflower was a place I could go to be safe from myself. Where professionals could make sure I took my meds and got enough rest to restore me to sanity. A place that would shield me from the pressures of the outside world. It was a good place, supposedly.

On day one I met Annabel. My roommate. Annabel was bipolar and a self-harmer, and had been there awhile by the time I showed up. She had earned the privilege of a CD player and one CD, *Spiceworld*. That first night when I started crying—how had I ended up somewhere so dismal? Would I ever get out?—she pressed PLAY. It wasn't the Spice Girls that cheered me up, but the idea that there was someone in the world who wanted to cheer me. She had scars up and down her arms, but I didn't see that. I just saw her big brown eyes and the dreamy, beguiled shine they got when she looked at me. Nobody had ever looked at me like that, like I was valid, like I was desirable, and it made me want to be around her all the time.

So we spent as much time together as possible, pulled and stuck like magnets. She was so pretty, with curly, honey-brown hair, and deep dimples in her tan cheeks. We watched *Veronica Mars* reruns in the community room, snuck cigarettes from the older kids out in the courtyard, stayed up late reading tarot cards and giving them our own meanings. We never discussed where we'd come from or where we wanted to go. We were in the moment. We *were* the moment. We made sure to never kiss or even touch in public; if they found us out they'd put us in separate rooms.

You have to have lost touch with reality to get admitted into Bellflower, but once you're there, reality gets further away. You have psychiatrists tinkering with your medications and no interactions with the outside world. You get very little sunlight and way too much sleep. You have nurses and orderlies forcing you to fall in line with rules that feel arbitrary, telling you you're not well enough to make your own decisions, that your free will has been taken away from you for a good reason. Lights out at eight even if you're not tired, wake up at five even if you are.

They watch you playing checkers like you plan on filing down one of the pieces to slit your throat; they peer under your tongue, under your bed, checking for any stowed-away relics of your freedom. You ask when you'll be able to go home, but they won't tell you. You forget your family. They're not coming to visit. Especially Annabel's, as it turned out. They were dead.

The Plan was born out of desperation. Living in the

moment, it turns out, can start to feel like hell. If you're always in the moment and the moment is distinguished by browns and grays of all shades, food that tastes like nothing, beds that are more wire than mattress, with papery sheets they only wash once a month, it becomes somewhere you want to escape.

The security was high at Bellflower, so we knew we couldn't just slip out. And we felt we wanted to preserve ourselves, be together forever on another plane of reality. I'd heard somewhere that death isn't real. It's like, we're all on channel four, and when someone dies they go to channel five. It's not that they stop existing, we just can't see them because they're on another channel. I said this to Annabel and she said, "Wanna change the channel?"

And so we had a plan. And it felt good to have a plan, to store the pills away until we had enough for both of us. It brought us even closer, this teamwork, and I felt more and more committed to it every day. I honestly had no idea that I'd change my mind.

✳ ✳ ✳

"Justine?" Dr. Morton asked again. "Are you paying attention?"

"Sorry, what was the question?"

"On a scale from one to ten, how high would you rate your worst panic attack?"

I remembered my last night with Annabel and said, "Ten."

✳ ✳ ✳

I'd imagined court would be this regal, sort of majestic place. Marble hallways and Grecian columns, mahogany tables and podiums and balconies, even. Like Atticus Finch could appear any minute and throw an apple or whatever at the defendant, thus restoring justice and peace and balance to civilization itself. But it was nothing like that.

The airport courthouse is called that because it's right next to Los Angeles International Airport. You can see planes taking off and landing so close it looks like you could reach out and touch them, people going places, people returning home safely, the radical heat of jet fuel rippling from the engines looking like a mirage, like wormholes in the sky. From the ninth floor you can see cars down on the freeway below veering from their lanes just slightly as they round the bends. I stood near the windows—unreasonably large, braced with diagonal iron beams—daydreaming about the airplanes, pretending to be a passenger on my way to a normal life. On my way to college, maybe, on the East Coast, where nobody knew my name. What was so bad about being anonymous? Why had I gnawed my way out of that life?

My mom sat on a bench somewhere behind me,

making phone call after phone call. I couldn't imagine who she was speaking to, but each call sounded just as much a matter of life and death as the last. The hallway we waited in was goose-bump cold and generically carpeted in smooth, dense gray. I watched a digital clock hung up on a sunburned-looking wall climbing in slow motion from eight to eight thirty to almost nine before a door finally opened and Jack ushered us into the courtroom.

The ceilings were low and paneled and perforated with tiny holes, fluorescent lights embedded throughout, buzzing. The seats were plastic and folded up like in a movie theater, and completely unoccupied. Nobody was here to see this movie. This bland, uninspired movie of my life, where District Attorney Melinda Warren would try to claim I should be tried, not just for a crime I didn't commit, but as an adult. This bitch actually wanted me to take adult responsibility for something she had no real proof I was guilty of.

Melinda Warren was tall, poised, young. She wore a tan pantsuit, her honey-blond hair in a chignon. She was so beautiful. Plump lips and arched eyebrows, pastel-blue eyes, subtle dimples, and a beauty mark resting on the upper right quadrant of her left cheek. Dime-sized pearls in her ears. She crossed her arms and held my gaze. *One way or another*—I swallowed—*this woman is going to end me.*

"Well," she said when she saw me enter, "look who it is. Whiplash girl child in the flesh."

"Justine, this is Assistant District Attorney Melinda Warren. She's prosecuting the case. Melinda, this is my client, Justine Childs."

"Oh, I know who you are," she said, not so much *to* me as *at* me. "You slayed your best friend in cold blood."

"All right, that's enough, Melinda." Jack held up a hand. "Let's not, okay?"

The judge—a rubbery, bland-looking man with black-rimmed glasses—entered and took a seat at his podium. A placard in black-and-gold read: Judge Marshall Brandeis. "All rise," he said. We rose. "Fitness hearing number 7715," he read, a little too drowsily for my liking. "We'll be determining if Justine Childs is fit to be tried as an adult for the crime of murder in the second degree. You may be seated."

We sat. Coffee sloshed back and forth in my empty stomach. I wondered if I'd ever have an appetite again. *Murder in the second degree.* Probably not.

"I'm ready to hear from the people," he said. "DA Warren?"

"Yes, your honor." Melinda stood. "The crime committed here was no accident, nor was it the act of a child. Eva-Kate Kelly was stabbed with a dagger and left to bleed to death. Justine Childs is sixteen years of age, fully old enough to be tried as an adult. She spent the summer without parental supervision, taking care of herself, party hopping with socialites and celebrities. The life she's been living is hardly that of a child. The people ask that this case be moved to adult court, where it belongs."

She sat down and crossed her long legs. I fixed my eyes on Judge Brandeis, looking for a hint of what he was thinking. Had she swayed him? He kept a poker face and extended an open hand in Jack's direction. "Mr. Willoughby?"

"Thank you, your honor." Jack stood, and I relaxed immediately. "I'd like to start by pointing out that my client is being completely misrepresented both by the tabloids and by Miss Warren. Yes, she spent a week or two without supervision, but that is only because she has a reputation for being well behaved and trust-worthy. She's a straight-A student without any record of delinquent behavior whatsoever. She plays cello in her school's symphony orchestra, and is known in her neighborhood as a friendly and reliable dog walker. She has her own dog, Princess Leia, with whom she has a loving bond. Everything we know about Justine points to her being a compassionate and harmless person. She's a *good* kid, your honor, but more importantly she *is a kid*, and trying her as an adult would be inappropriate and a huge mistake." He sat down and gave me a confident nod.

"Would the defense or prosecution like to call forth any witnesses?"

"Your honor." Jack stood again. "I'd like to call Dr. Daniel Morton, the psychiatrist who assessed Miss Childs's fitness for juvenile court."

This will be good, I thought, *I did a perfect job convincing him.*

When Dr. Morton took the stand, I looked up at him with wide doe eyes, praying he'd see me for what I really was, or at least for what I really wanted to be: a kid. In that moment nothing seemed as gruesome or as tragic as crossing over into adulthood.

"Dr. Morton," Jack questioned, "did you get the opportunity to interview Miss Childs and come up with an assessment as to whether or not she's fit to be tried in adult court?"

"I did, yes."

"And what did you find?"

"I found that though Miss Childs is highly intelligent, and although the crime she's accused of is quite severe in nature, she lacks both the mental and emotional maturity to be tried as an adult. Additionally, she would be benefitted greatly by the rehabilitation programs offered to those convicted in juvenile court."

"And what was that assessment based on?"

"Several factors. Primarily: She has had no history of violence or drug abuse, and despite a few brief and uncharacteristic weeks spent attending parties with Eva-Kate Kelly, she has zero experience living life as an adult. She relies on her parents for food and shelter, and she relies on her school friends and classmates for a sense of community. Being sixteen, her brain isn't fully developed, nor is it capable of understanding reality on an adult level."

"Thank you, Dr. Morton. No further questions, your honor."

"Dr. Morton, you may step down," said the judge. Dr. Morton stepped down.

That's it? I thought as Judge Brandeis began jotting notes. *That's all there is to say to determine my fate?* Neither of them was wrong, I realized, but neither was right either. I was eleven when I started wondering about my status as a child, twelve when I started doubting I could identify as one. But when you're thirteen and your friends start hosting parties and ceremonies to mark the beginning of their "womanhood," when you're fourteen and Kyle Reed from fourth-period symphony orchestra puts his hand up your skirt and you don't do anything to stop him, your doubt becomes a full-blown identity crisis. I'd spent so many nights in front of the mirror wondering who I was, who I'd become, now that I wasn't a kid anymore. But one thing was for sure: I wouldn't survive a week in the adult prison system. I shifted nervously in the dark depths of the unknown.

"All rise," Judge Brandeis commanded. I felt wobbly on my legs and pressed my palms on the table to steady myself. "From what I've heard, Justine Childs is unfit to stand trial in juvenile court. She will be tried as an adult."

I gasped.

District Attorney Warren smirked.

"Your honor—" Jack tried, but was interrupted.

"Mr. Willoughby, if your client is, in fact, innocent, she has a better chance of being proven so by a jury," said Judge Brandeis. "She's sixteen and of sound mind and body; there's no reason to try her as a juvenile. Court adjourned."

He banged his gavel and got up to leave. Jack's shoulders sagged.

"See you in court." Warren wiggled her fingers at us and strode out, the double doors swinging behind her as she left.

✷ ✷ ✷

"What did he mean that I have a better chance being proven innocent by a jury?" I asked. It was a new day and I found myself back in Jack's office. My mom had to ply me with Xanax and bribe me with ice cream to get me there, and once she had, she'd fled to tend to a patient, shaking Jack's hand as if to say *she's your problem now.*

"Even though the stakes are much lower in juvenile court, the chances that one judge will find you guilty are much higher than for twelve civilians who have to agree on a verdict. A jury will be less likely to agree on your guilt, and so you do have a better chance of getting an innocent verdict."

"But if they do vote guilty, I could go to jail for . . . the rest of my life . . ." I had intended this to be a question, but it trailed off at the end as I saw myself behind bars, wrinkled and weathered and wasting away.

"And we'll cross that bridge *if* we get to it, but in the meantime let's just focus on winning, okay?"

"Mhm," I mumbled. I tried to picture myself any-where other than behind bars. I tried to picture myself free, on an island somewhere with a syrup-heavy mojito and a warm breeze and the sting of sand and sun and salt water where no one would ever find me.

"As I've said, I'm going to be arguing that there isn't enough evidence to prove your guilt. Once I show how thin the prosecution's case is, no way will the jury vote to convict. I mean, I can't promise that. But I think it looks good. I want to start by filling in some blanks. The only real glitch here is the timeline." The weight he put into these words unnerved me. It confirmed what I already feared: The timeline was more than just a glitch.

"The timeline," I said, as if saying it could put off having to talk about it.

"According to the coroner's report, Eva-Kate Kelly died between midnight and four in the morning. You weren't at the Ace Hotel until five, which means technically you could have . . . you could have committed the crime."

"But I *didn't*."

"You don't need to convince me."

"Don't I?"

"No, Justine," he said. "You really don't, okay? You need to convince the jury. And in order to do that, we need to hear from you what happened and where you were leading up to your arrival at the Ace."

"Great. I'm ready. Now? Should I tell you now?"

He uncapped a Uni-ball. "Go slowly so I can get it all down."

I sighed deeply. "We got home from San Luis Obispo at 9:00 P.M. Eva-Kate and I. While she was downstairs talking to Josie and London and Olivia, I went upstairs to put my stuff away. That's when I heard the landline ringing. To my *great surprise*, and quite frankly, horror, the person calling was my own mom, letting Eva-Kate know that she'd be back in town soon and they could restart their sessions."

"Your mom is Eva-Kate's therapist?"

"She was. But I didn't know it until that moment."

"Eva-Kate never told you?"

"No."

"And your mom never told you?"

"Also no."

"Huh." He chewed lightly on the pen cap. "That's strange, isn't it?"

"Thank you. It's extremely strange."

"But I don't know what to make of it."

"Me neither. It feels like it should be relevant, but I don't know how."

"We'll get back to it. Go on."

"So then I confronted Eva-Kate, and she acted like it wasn't weird at all. She lied and said my mom had given her her blessing to buy the house basically across the street, which is just really creepy because I know for a fact my mom did not."

"How do you know that?"

"Because if she had known Eva-Kate was moving in, my mom wouldn't have left me alone there for the summer. I mean, sure, she wanted me to go stay with Aunt Jillian, but if she knew Eva-Kate was moving to Carroll Canal, she would have *for sure* lectured me about staying away from her. My mom is obsessed with me not getting into trouble. Or she was. That ship has kinda sailed now."

"Then what happened?"

"I felt really freaked out. I don't know exactly what I was scared of, I just knew something was really off. Like, *really* off. This girl had lied to me all summer, she'd known my mom was her therapist and hadn't said anything about it, and she'd moved across the street from her therapist. Without telling her. That's not a good sign. It's not a sign of sanity, that's for sure. I didn't feel safe, so I had to leave. I had to figure out what the hell was going on. So I went home and broke into my mom's file cabinets, which is when I learned that Eva-Kate had been seeing my mom for many years, and that she had this strange fixation with me and my life—"

"Wait, how did you get into the cabinets?"

"Trial and error," I said. "I guessed the passcode. I got it wrong a few times, but eventually I guessed right. It was Eva-Kate's birthday. 061300."

"Eva-Kate's birthday? Why? Have you asked your mom about it?"

"She said she set the code years and years ago when Eva-Kate was a kid, something about wanting to cheer her up."

"Do you believe that?"

"I don't know. Does it matter?"

"It could. Making the code to her cabinet Eva-Kate's birthday is . . . intense. Is it possible . . . Well, I'm just wondering if—I'm sorry, there's no delicate way to say this."

"You can just say it. I really don't mind."

"I'm wondering if your mom had any kind of

unhealthy fixation with Eva-Kate. And if she did, is it possible that she killed her?"

"Obviously I've thought about that," I said, "but I can't think of a motive. A fixation? Do people really kill out of fixation? My mom is nuts, but I don't see her as the type to be driven to murder by a teenager."

"Okay, so you were saying"—he read from his notes— "you learned that Eva-Kate had been seeing your mom for many years and that she had this strange fixation with your life."

"Right, which is utterly insane, because my life has never been at all interesting. Aside from Bellflower, but that was so brief. But she was intrigued by me being so normal—or so *real*—or something like that. She thought I was a real girl in a fake plastic world, and she needed to know me because of that. Which is so sad, I mean, that she was so deprived of down-to-earth people that she actually thought *I* was. And the thing is, I'm *not*, I've never been down to earth. I was just grounded compared to the flighty airheads that surrounded her. And I guess she was hungry for that. For substance. It's just so sad how wrong she was. About me. And I guess how wrong I was about her."

Jack Willoughby scribbled furiously as I talked. I peered at his sheet of paper and saw he had written down every single word I'd said. "So then what?" He came up for air.

"I knew my mom was going to be home soon, and I didn't want to see her or talk to her. It was just so insanely creepy knowing that the two of them had known each other since I was a kid. *This whole time*, I just kept thinking, *this whole time*. I took it too personally. I thought maybe they were, like, conspiring against me, which I know sounds crazy, but I hadn't gotten a lot of sleep and I, well, I wasn't like completely up to date on my meds, and after all they were both keeping a secret from me, so in a way I had reason to be paranoid. I think. Maybe."

"Go on . . ."

"I realized I had all this money from my Hot Toxic hair dye contract so I took an Uber to the Ace."

"Why the Ace?"

"I've just always wanted to go." I shrugged.

"How long were you at your mom's? From when to when?"

"I don't know," I sighed. "I know I left around four thirty in the morning. And I guess I must have gotten there around 10:00 P.M. Six and a half hours? I was definitely there at my mom's during the window where they say Eva-Kate, you know, died."

"Can you think of anyone, anyone at all, who can vouch for that?"

"No." I closed my eyes. My neck fought to keep the enormous weight of my head upright. "Nobody was home and nobody was around. Nobody saw me."

"Okay, so run me through it one more time. I know, I know, it's tedious, but bear with me for just a second. You got back to Eva-Kate's around nine, so you confronted her about the voice mail around when, nine thirty?"

"Sure. Yeah. Nine thirty-ish. Look, Jack, what good is any of this if we can't give the jury . . . I mean, I know for a fact I'd feel much better if we had a working alternative theory . . . something that doesn't just plant some doubt in the jury's mind, but something that makes them fully confident in my innocence."

"Well—"

"In the Bianchi sisters' case that you won, you were able to prove that somebody else was in the house and it unraveled the whole thing! I know there were other people at Eva-Kate's that night, people who were there long after I left, even."

"And you think one of them could be the guilty party."

"Of course. Dr. Silver, her plastic surgeon, came by that night, did you know that? London saw him. I'm sure you can check the surveillance footage. I mean, why in God's name would a doctor show up at—"

"But his fingerprints weren't on the weapon."

"Okay, but maybe . . . maybe he wore gloves! He's a doctor, after all."

"Possible," said Jack. "But if we're narrowing it down to realistic suspects, we should focus on people who did leave fingerprints on the athame."

"You mean besides mine? *They found matches?*" I

almost jumped out of my chair but dug my nails into the leather arms to restrain myself.

"Yep." Jack opened a manila folder and read from its contents. "Rob Donovan, Liza McKelvoy, Olivia Law, and Josie Bishop."

"Are you kidding me?" I pulled my cheeks down with my palms. "Then it could have been any one of them. God, I'm so stupid. I believed them when they said they didn't do it."

"Who said they didn't do it? Who did you talk to?"

"All of them," I said. "You know, Rob and Liza are missing. Nobody knows where they are. Isn't that suspicious? And they had motive. Eva-Kate was blackmailing—"

"Hold on. It *would* look suspicious, yes, but their alibis check out. The doorman at Rob's building says they were there all night."

"Then it was Josie," I said. "It had to be Josie."

CHAPTER 13

JUSTINE CHILDS WRITES A POEM

*I*t had to be Josie, but I couldn't prove it. I spent weeks trying to figure it out as preparations for trial continued around me. It was April when I stopped trying. I just didn't have any energy left. My fate closed in around me, black and blotchy and cold. The fright of it was oppressive, paralyzing. Most days I didn't bother to get out of bed.

I woke every morning feeling steamrolled. My eyes sagged and stung, lids heavy and drooping, sinuses swollen. Eating became a laborious chore, and I lost seven pounds. Showering felt utterly inconceivable, so I dragged myself into the bath and lay there for hours wasting the day, wasting away. I hoped to stay in the water so long my skin and bones would dissolve and disappear down the drain, but eventually I always got interrupted. My mom would knock, saying she needed the bathroom, so I'd wrap myself in a towel, throw myself onto the bed, and lovingly examine the deep, waterlogged grooves in my fingertips.

Taylor Swift started teasing the world with clues about her new album and I started losing my mind trying to crack the code. I wrote about it in an attempt to regain my sanity.

It is uncomfortable waiting with the masses,
 feeling
like a sheep, watching the clock count down
 until
God knows what.
You want to say:
YOUR SOLAR FLARES ARE FAKE, YOUR
 PASTELS ARE MANIPULATIVE, but
there's a too-sweet pulse thwacking in your
 veins, pooling in your gut telling you
it's all as real
and as genuine
as the moment you wake up in the morning
and know that one of these days it'll be for the
 last time.

All day you're thinking about me.
Not the me that is you, but the me

that is Taylor Swift. The real me. Owning a
*   decadent collection of flaws*
and calling them gems. Asking
for the spotlight and wearing it comfortably
like a second skin.
That me is buried somewhere under backlot
*   cobblestone pastel*
and years of shedding snakeskin
turned to butterflies
turned to dust.

At the stroke of midnight Eastern
you sneak away in search of reception and
*   find it outside*
in the Los Angeles concept of cold
by a congregation of valet-parked Maseratis
packed in tight, perched and silken
like a murder of crows. You hold the phone to
*   your ear*
and you shiver as you listen for the First Time
*   thinking*
where, God, please tell me where, does this
*   confidence come from?*
And how does one find a place in this world
*   among*
the warring colors of a rainbow and the
nonstop
nonchalance

of all the cool chicks out there?
You think why is Taylor Swift 29 and still
    fighting in the rain? which really means:
Why have I never fought in the rain? Why
    have I never kissed
in the rain?
A flower doesn't compare itself
to the flower standing next to it, it just grows.
    What a lovely sentiment, you say to
    nobody, but
do I look like a fucking flower to you?

You go home and watch the Music Video on
    repeat, looking for a sign
that Taylor Swift is the all-knowing,
the unmoved mover, the puppet master who
    pulled
the strings of these cosmos together once upon
    a time.
A sign that you should pledge allegiance,
    swallow a handful of
Easter eggs and sidewalk chalk
and feel it feel so good, warming the neon
    passageways to your heart
and feel it feel like home.

I hate when people talk about "real love." As if there is fake love. My thesis: All love is real.

There are so many different ways to love. But right now there are two types on my mind: the kind that is pure and the kind that is obsession. There is love that is pure obsession. Someone else might try to tell you otherwise, but ask me and I'll tell you that obsession is a kind of love. This is how I love Taylor Swift, in obsession form. And this form comes from curiosity that can't possibly be satisfied. When curiosity can't be satisfied it grows until it becomes obsession. I want to know what Taylor thinks about—what does she think of herself, for starters? Does she see herself as a poet, or as a commodity? Does she feel larger than life? Does she get to experience that larger than life-ness? What does it feel like when you can't leave your home without a swarm of paparazzi and fans who have come from all over the world to get a look at you? Does that feel good? Do you come to understand yourself as special? What does being a real, true, breathing human being become when impacted by the intricate pressures of mass superstardom? What happens to the inside of that brain? I want to climb in, wander through the periwinkle mechanisms and make sense of it all. But I can't.

I can try to understand Taylor Swift—what it means to be sensitive yet brave, vulnerable yet powerful—but I'll never understand. The good people at Bellflower would say, "If you can't change it, you might as well accept it." Accept the things you cannot change. But I can't accept. And so I obsess.

This, too, is the way I love Eva-Kate. I stay up late with wind chime ruminations. If she had lived, if she were alive right now, would I be able to figure her out? Understand the hallways, the ballrooms, the spiral staircases of her mind? Would I have ever been able to untangle her? See the world the way she saw the world, see me the way she saw me? I'll never know. Because she's gone, understanding Eva-Kate Kelly is even more impossible than understanding Taylor Swift. I'll never know. Sometimes I'll think about it long enough that it feels as though I'm getting close to some kind of answer, but just as I go to reach it, it becomes vapor, and I plummet. My curiosity, unsatisfied, becomes a fire.

On the other end of the spectrum, there is love that is bred from profound understanding. This is the way I love Lana Del Rey. You might think I love Taylor Swift more than I love Lana Del Rey, but you'd be wrong. I am obsessed with Taylor Swift, but I am satisfied by Lana Del Rey. She makes sense to me. Almost too much sense. I see myself in her. I see her as a better, enhanced, evolved version of myself. I knew her in a past life and I will know her in the next one. This I know. And this is pure love. Pure love is warm, it holds you. Obsessed love is cold, it locks you out. Both are real. Both rule my life.

It was obsessed love that brought Ruby into my life.

My mom thought Ruby was trouble, but she said Ruby could keep me company as long as we stayed in the house. Ruby brought me crystals and tinctures. Aventurine and bloodstone for luck and energy, passionflower and valerian tea to heal my nerves and anxiety. None of it worked, but having her there had a calming effect. When I asked her why she was being so good to me, she said, "Because I trust you. You were probably the only one of Eva-Kate's friends who wasn't using her. Plus, I know she loved you and would want me to take care of you." But that made me feel a lot worse.

Ruby, only three years older than me, had seen every episode of *Law & Order: SVU*. I'd never even seen one, and this horrified her. So we started at the beginning and worked our way through season one on my laptop. I didn't think I'd be able to handle the gore, the disturbing perversions, but it turned out I could. Actually, there was something oddly comforting about the whole thing, something about those brutal and savage sex crimes packaged so cleanly into forty-minute episodes that helped soothe me to sleep way better than aventurine or bloodstone or passionflower or valerian ever could. I hoped that didn't make me some kind of creep or psycho. Ruby told me not to feel guilty.

"There's a reason *SVU* is going into its twentieth season," she said. "People fucking love it." So it wasn't just me.

I tried to figure out why the name Detective Olivia Benson sounded so familiar, and finally realized during "Wanderlust" (season one, episode five). In 2014, Taylor

Swift went on *The Ellen Show* and told the world about her new cat, who she named after her favorite character on *Law & Order: SVU*, Detective Olivia Benson. "I sit in my apartment and watch hours of that show," she'd said in a *Teen Vogue* interview three years earlier. "So I sort of feel like me and Olivia are BFFs."

It wasn't just me, and it wasn't just the vast *SVU* fan base, but it was also Taylor Swift. If Taylor Swift watched hours of these lurid storylines, then there couldn't be something wrong with me for doing the same thing. Or at least nobody could say there was.

So I watched through a new lens. The *Taylor Swift has seen this* lens. All I kept thinking was how outrageous it was; all along, this whole time, sweet, adorable Taylor Swift has been binge-watching a show about New York's most elaborately cruel sex crimes. The thought was so outrageous to me I had to laugh. Then I had to explain it all to Ruby.

"I mean, she's Taylor Swift, she doesn't live here in this world with us. She lives in a protective bubble designed to shield her from all that is grim, to keep her safe and pure. She doesn't know about rape and murder, she doesn't know about incest or pedophilia or kidnapping or torture or even death. Except it turns out she *does*. She does, and she binge-watches it!"

"What an epic reveal," said Ruby. Of course she wasn't as excited about it as I was, but I think she understood.

Taylor Swift knows about death. She isn't immune to the world's iniquities after all. She may have four or five multimillion-dollar homes to hear about it all from, but she hears about it.

✶ ✶ ✶

One week in and we needed a break from the nonstop tragedy of *Law & Order: SVU*. Ruby made popcorn and valerian tea and we watched *Bring It On* in the living room after my mom had gone to bed.

"You know, I've never once seen a cheerleader in real life. I wouldn't be even a little surprised if they turned out to be mythical." She handed me my cup of tea, some of it spilling out onto her silk pajama sleeves.

"Oh, they're real. Unfortunately," I assured her. "You'd have seen one by now if you'd ever set foot on a school campus."

"*School.*" She rolled her eyes. "Gross. My greatest accomplishment in life was dodging that bullet."

"Have you really never gone to school?"

"No." She sipped her tea. "I did go to school. For a while. Once upon a time. But let me tell you all you need to know about school, Justine. The last time I was there, just three years ago, there was a Hemingway imitation contest. You had to submit a piece of writing in Hemingway's style. I submitted an *actual Hemingway poem* and got first place."

"What do you mean?" I laughed. "How?"

"I submitted a poem *actually written by Hemingway* and none of the teachers noticed. It went like, 'If my Valentine you won't be / I'll hang myself on your Christmas tree.' Can you believe that?"

"That was the *whole poem*?" I thought it had to be the dumbest thing I'd ever heard.

"Yeah." She giggled. "I guess I can see why they thought a kid wrote it. But still, I can't waste my life in an institution like that. I mean, I don't know which is worse, the fact that they couldn't recognize Hemingway's work when they saw it, or the fact that they came up with the contest in the first place. I mean, please, *Hemingway*? He's the easiest writer to imitate. Fuck that. Fuck Hemingway."

It was our eighth night together, I counted, when Ruby fell asleep before me. I used my phone to google "what kind of cat is Detective Olivia Benson." It turns out she's a purebred Scottish fold, which cost about one thousand five hundred dollars to buy from a breeder. I swiped through hundreds of pictures that night. Olivia licking Taylor's MTV Video Music Award, Olivia on Taylor Swift's couch, Olivia in Taylor Swift's shoe, Olivia posing next to Taylor Swift's *1989* vinyl, Olivia in an accidental yoga pose, Olivia slouched grumpily on a paisley armchair, Olivia as a newborn kitten on Taylor Swift's lap, Olivia on Taylor Swift's shoulder in a Coke commercial, Olivia on a car ride, Olivia as a giant cardboard cutout, Olivia as a giant unicorn (aka Caticorn) in a DirecTV commercial, Olivia asleep on Taylor Swift's private jet, Olivia perched on Taylor Swift's arm as she's leaving her New York apartment.

At first the images were a sweet dulling of the anxiety sharpening and sharpening like a shiv in my side, but as I went on I realized this cat was living a categorically better life than I was, or than I ever would, and the anxiety morphed into a blue knot of melancholy that pulsed in me like a second heart. I had always been like that. Jealous of anyone and anything, even a cat.

I clicked on the picture of Taylor Swift leaving her apartment and was taken to an article about the many homes she's purchased over the years. In 2009, at the age of twenty, she bought a 4,062-square-foot penthouse apartment in Nashville for $2 million. *Vulture* described it as "whimsically girlie" with a style that resembles a "shabby-chic Alice in Wonderland." In 2011 she bought a Cape Cod–style home in Beverly Hills for $3.97 million. The 2,826-square-foot house includes four bedrooms, four bathrooms, and a tennis court. In 2013, she bought an 11,000-square-foot Rhode Island mansion for $17.75 million. She paid for it in cash. In 2016, she started renting a $40,000 a month townhouse in Manhattan's West Village while she renovated the two penthouse floors in Tribeca. She bought the penthouse floors from *Lord of the Rings* director Peter Jackson for $20 million. I did the math and found that when all is said and done, Taylor Swift has spent $44 million buying homes across the country. And that's not even counting the two she bought for her parents.

I tried to make myself feel happy for her, but instead I just keep thinking that I might spend the rest of my life behind bars—showering with strangers, squatting pantsless in front of guards to make sure I wasn't hiding drugs inside my body—while Taylor Swift moved into her two-story penthouse that she bought for $20 million from *Lord of the Rings* director Peter Jackson. By the time I put my phone down, the sun was starting to rise. *The sun also rises*, I thought, and fell asleep.

✱ ✱ ✱

On the tenth night in a row we hung out together, Ruby was covering my body in crystals, the curtains open so that the crystals could be charged by the moon, when suddenly she said, "I wonder why she texted him that night."

"Who?" I asked, trying to stay very still so the crystals wouldn't fall off me.

"Dr. Silver. He said the night she died she texted him and told him to come over. But when he got there nobody came to the door. I wonder why she asked him to come over. Were they . . . I mean, if Eva-Kate had been sleeping with an older man, we would have known about it.

So that can't be it. Do you think she was like, *scared*, or something?"

There had been the voice mail left by my mom. Eva-Kate knew I'd heard it. Was it me she'd been afraid of? Afraid that I'd found out? No, that didn't quite make sense. What would Dr. Silver have been able to do about that anyway? I wondered if I should say any of this out loud, tell Ruby about my mom and Eva-Kate, but I decided it didn't make me look good. It gave me a reason to be mad at Eva-Kate, and I couldn't afford anyone seeing me in that light.

"Nobody came to the door," I said instead. "But the house *wasn't* empty. London had to have been there if she saw him come over."

"Right, *London*." Ruby's head bobbed. "London had to have been there. How else could she have known he came by?"

"You said Olivia couldn't have done it because she faints at the sight of blood, but what about London?"

"London's a tough bitch. Tough and dumb. I just don't know *why* she'd do it. No motive."

"Dr. Silver said the top three reasons people kill are revenge, jealousy, and greed. I read once that the fourth is power. Maybe London was tired of being bossed around, talked down to."

"I don't know, is that really reason enough to murder your friend?"

"I don't know." I shrugged, and the two rose quartz stones resting on my collarbones clattered to the floor. "It is if you're crazy."

"Was London crazy?"

"I don't know." I sat up and let all the crystals fall away, then pulled on my robe. "I didn't know her long enough."

"I didn't really know her either," said Ruby. "I knew her the least of Eva-Kate's friends. Frankly I think she was Eva-Kate's least favorite."

"Do you know why?"

"She was the least interesting."

It was true. I hadn't been particularly interested in her either. I was now.

"Doesn't matter," said Ruby. "It had to be Debbie. Or Liza. Or maybe both. That's why they ran."

"Rob's gone too, now," I said. "I don't know what I think anymore."

Ruby sighed. "Did you ever feel like . . . ," she said, then paused, massaging her jaw. "Did you ever feel like you didn't know the real Eva-Kate? Like, even when she was in her most vulnerable moments, there was still a whole sea beneath the surface that she refused to show?"

"Sure," I said. "But, you know, she didn't think she had anything real beneath the surface anymore."

"What do you mean?"

"Oh." I scraped nervously at my cuticles, wanting to go back in time. I had assumed anything Eva-Kate told me she had also told Ruby, but maybe I'd been wrong. "I mean, nothing. It's just this one time she mentioned that because she'd been in front of the spotlight for so long, you know, performing her whole life, that the real her had been like, banished, or something. She was worried she'd never get it back. She worried she looked like a real human girl, but that anything real about her had been dissolved."

"'Fake Plastic Trees,'" Ruby said then, nodding. "She always said that song was about her."

"Do you think she was right? About herself, I mean."

"I didn't know her like you did," I offered. "But no, I don't. Maybe something fundamentally real and true about her had been cut off or warped by fame, but it was still there. She had pain, you know? So she had a soul."

"*Did* she have pain, though? Or was she just a really good actress?"

"She was a really good actress," I said. "But not *that* good. And why would she pretend to be in pain if she wasn't?"

"Duh," said Ruby. "To seem more real."

"If she was really a shell of a person pretending to have human emotions, that would make her a sociopath."

"Well, she might have been. Maybe that's what got her killed. Maybe she was having too much fun manipulating people just to feel alive and finally someone had enough of it. Maybe she was toying with Dr. Silver for sport and he just lost it."

Was she toying with me for sport? I wondered. *Toying with my mom? Was what I read in her notes the truth or just a sociopath's fabrication?*

"Justine?" Ruby asked when a minute had passed and I hadn't responded. "Are you okay?"

"Yeah, sorry." I shook the thoughts loose from my mind. "I just have this tendency to . . . it's just really easy for me to lose sight of reality. I get disoriented."

"I get that," said Ruby. "Who's to say what's real, anyway? Once I stayed up too many nights on Crimsons and was convinced that all of what we see on Earth is a hallucination. I started scratching at the walls as if actual reality lay behind it." She laughed. "After I broke a few nails I tried to check myself into the psych ward."

"Tried?" I asked. "What happened?"

"The doctor who did my intake made me go home. Apparently I wasn't psych ward material. He said I just needed to sleep. I'm glad they didn't admit me. Apparently life in a psych ward isn't as glamorous as you'd think."

"It's not," I said. "I spent some time at Bellflower, actually."

"No way." Her eyes lit up. "Why?"

"I'm not really sure. I think it started as some kind of manic episode. I didn't sleep for a while, I don't know how many days exactly, and then I got it in my head that me staying up was the only thing keeping the Earth in orbit. I thought I had to stay up to make sure the sun rose in the morning and set at night." I covered my mouth, it sounded so ridiculous, even more ridiculous out loud than in my mind. But Ruby just nodded.

"That's wild," she said.

"I don't know why I'm telling you this," I said. "I've never told anybody before."

"Big deal." Ruby shrugged. "We're all mad here."

"I had a girlfriend there," I blurted, some kind of floodgate opening up inside me. "At Bellflower. Annabel."

"Oh?" I couldn't tell if she was impressed or judging my outburst. "Where is she now?"

"She's dead," I said, smiling in spite of myself. I guess it just felt good to share.

* * *

On the eleventh night I woke up around 3:00 A.M. and found Ruby packing her crystals into a Gucci Mini Marmont backpack. Her hair was tied back in a silk headscarf and she had her shoes on.

"Where are you going?" I asked.

"The natives are getting restless," she said. "I have to get back to them."

"The natives?" I rubbed my eyes.

"You know, Zander and the others."

"Hey, Ruby?" I sat up.

"Hm?"

"Are they, like . . . enslaved to you?"

She laughed quietly and hooked a self-conscious finger over her top lip.

"To be enslaved is to have no freedom of choice," she said. "They want to be with me. They're boys who need to be controlled in order to feel safe. And I need to be in control in order to feel safe. It's a good arrangement we have. Symbiosis. See? I told you I don't need school."

Then, just like that, she was gone. In the morning it was as if she'd never been there at all.

CHAPTER 14

THE PEOPLE VS. JUSTINE CHILDS: ALL THE JUICY DETAILS

*T*he thing about fame is that people care about you. Even if they don't know you, they care what you're doing or not doing, who you're dating, where you're going, what you're going to do next. In fact, the less they truly know you, the more they care about those things. You become relevant, a subject of thought and specula-tion in the homes of people you've never met. I'd wanted that gift for so long but didn't see how I could ever get it. I didn't know a second-degree-murder charge would do the trick. There wasn't a single tabloid cover on the stands without my face on it.

I walked behind Jack Willoughby up the courthouse steps, both my parents following close behind me. I wore a royal-blue Prada skirt suit that Ruby let me borrow, with Manolo Blahnik shoes that rubbed against my heels as I walked, building blisters. Flashbulbs burst in every direction, microphones were thrust into my face, popping out from the crowd. I heard my name shouted over and over and over again, until it blended together, a mantra in my mind.

"Justine! What about the fingerprints? How do you explain the fingerprints?"

"Justine! Over here! How do you feel knowing you could go to jail?"

"Justine! What will you do next if you're found innocent?"

"Justine! When did you plan to murder Eva-Kate Kelly?"

"Justine! What do you have to say to your fans and supporters?"

"Justine! Who are you wearing?"

"Justine! What would you say to the people who think you're guilty?"

Justinejustinejustinejustinejustinejustine. I closed my eyes and saw only purple spots, hot and bright. At the top of the steps, Jack Willoughby turned around to face the crowd of reporters and paparazzi, who backed off slightly, holding out their microphones, holding up their cameras. I saw them as ants, scrambling frantically for a coveted bread crumb. I was that crumb.

"I won't be answering any questions." He held up his hands, saying *don't come any closer.* "But what I can say is that my client is innocent and has been wrongly accused. We've been looking forward to our day in court when we can finally prove that once and for all."

He pulled the courtroom door open and swept me in. When the eruption of questions was finally shut out, along with the lights and their inexhaustible pop-popping, I sighed deeply. I'd been holding my breath the entire way up.

✳ ✳ ✳

"All rise." Judge Victoria Lucas took her place at the podium, and the room rose to welcome her. She had orangey hair clipped beneath her chin in a blunt bob, her skin wrinkled and weathered. There was some-thing so reassuring about her presence. When I was twelve, my wisdom teeth grew in early, deeply impacted and unbearably painful. So they had to operate. I was terrified. I worried I'd go under the anesthesia and never come back. I worried the anesthesia wouldn't work at all and somehow I wouldn't be able to com-municate that to them, forcing me to endure every moment of agony, blades slicing into my gums, sev-ering roots. But the surgeon said I had nothing to be worried about.

"This is the most basic and routine procedure," he said. "And all in all it only takes twenty minutes. We've actually already done five this morning." It was only 9:00 A.M. His point was that he'd overseen the extraction of wisdom teeth more times than he could count, that it was so commonplace it almost bored him. That calmed me down enough to let them put me under.

Judge Victoria Lucas didn't say it out loud, but her face—her deep-set eyes and wrinkled mouth—conveyed a life of experience that told me I was being taken care of.

The room was packed. People overflowed from the benches, some choosing to stand, packed tight against the back wall. The jury were twelve people I didn't want to look at. I didn't want to know the faces of the people who were to decide my fate. If it went down badly, I'd spend the rest of my life haunted by them. Aside from my parents, the only familiar faces belonged to Riley and Ruby, and London and Olivia. Riley gave me a pathetic, pitying wave, and Ruby gave two thumbs up and then blew me a kiss, leaving a red imprint on her palm. London and Olivia didn't acknowledge me at all. Missing were Rob and Liza, Debbie, and Josie. *Where's Josie?* I wondered. She wouldn't miss this. Not on purpose, anyway. But of course, she must have been there. I just couldn't see her. She was waiting in the wings until it came time for her to testify against me.

"Docket ending 1270, the People versus Justine Childs," Judge Lucas recited, reading from a piece of paper through gold wire-rimmed glasses. "One count of murder in the second degree."

"Jack Willoughby for the defendant," Jack announced. As soon as we'd stepped into the courtroom, his body language changed. It went from tightly wound to loose and relaxed, almost swaggering, as if he'd entered his natural habitat and no longer had a single thing to worry about. *The courtroom is where I thrive*, he'd told me, *you'll see*. And now I was seeing. He wore a slender black silk tie that bisected him in half from his freckled neck down to his unwieldy belt buckle.

"ADA Melinda Warren for the people, your honor," said Melinda, shoulders pulled back and chin held high. She had an unnerving air of pure, distilled determination about her. The way she stood said *I am as permanent and unconquerable as the columns of ancient Greece.*

"You may be seated," Judge Lucas said. My muscles quivered, fatigued, as I tried to sit. "Does the prosecution wish to present an opening statement?"

"Yes, your honor, thank you." Melinda stood back up. Her legs were Barbie-doll long and sheathed in sheer beige nylon that shimmered in the light as she walked.

"The facts of the case are these: In the early morning hours of July seventeenth, 2018, Justine Childs stabbed her friend and neighbor Eva-Kate Kelly with a knife used for practicing *witchcraft*, then left her to bleed out in the Venice canals. This is a story of passion, of obsession, and of jealousy, the story of a stalker and her victim. This is the story you'll hear from Detectives Sato and Rayner, and it's the story you'll hear from Eva-Kate's lifelong best friend, Josie Bishop. Now, Mr. Willoughby is going to try to paint Miss Childs as a harmless sweetheart caught up with the wrong crowd. He's going to tell you stories of past rightdoing and good deeds. He won't have the supporting evidence, so he will invent reasons why she couldn't have possibly committed this heinous crime. But make no mistake, she did. The evidence shows that Justine Childs is a stone-cold killer, let's not forget that."

"Does the defense wish to make an opening statement?" Judge Lucas peered down over the tops of her half-moon glasses.

"Your honor," Jack began, using his spindly arms to push himself up from the table, "picture in your mind a young woman. No older than sixteen. She's a student, a daughter, and a friend. Her days are spent peacefully, uneventfully, taking care of the family dog and taking care of her parents' home while they're away on vacation. Until one day she has a new neighbor. Her new neighbor is fun, beautiful, intriguing, and famous. But, *more than that*, she is kind and welcoming. She invites this young woman into her world and brightens up her humdrum life by ten thousand percent. But, *more than that*, the two become close friends and confidants. Kindred spirits. Our young woman is finally enjoying life. *More than that*, she feels truly alive for the first time. Until, one night, an unspeakable tragedy occurs, and all of that is pulled right out from under her. Eva-Kate Kelly is not coming back. She was ripped from this life in a cruel act of violence. And now the prosecution is trying to lock up the last person on Earth who would or could have possibly done this awful deed. And, I might add, this charge was made following an investigation that was cursory at best, looking into a grand total of one suspect. So what Miss Warren has just illustrated for you is *not* the full story. In fact, what she has just spun for you is a fictional account of what happened that night. She says the evidence shows something that it simply does not. What the prosecution has against my client—namely, one piece of threadbare evidence and one unreliable witness—is circumstantial at best. And what the prosecution lacks—namely motive, hard evidence, and a definitive timeline—is quite significant. It absolutely cannot be proven beyond a reasonable doubt that my client did anything to harm Eva-Kate Kelly, and quite honestly, the true tragedy is that the real killer is still out there. Now, I can't tell you who that is, because, again, my client was the only person investigated. The irony is that there were many people who wanted to hurt Eva-Kate Kelly, but Justine Childs just wasn't one of them."

This isn't going to work. I felt it moving through my blood and my bones like a fog. *This isn't going to work.* If Jack's defense was that other people wanted to hurt her, wouldn't the judge need to know who? I studied Judge Lucas's face for signs of what she thought, but there was nothing there. She gave me nothing. I sweated underneath my borrowed blouse, the silk blend sticking to my skin.

Your honor, I have suspects. I wanted to run up to her podium and tell her everything I knew right then. *Your honor, Eva-Kate's closest friends resented her, she never trusted them and maybe she was right not to. Your honor, her Instagram feed is crawling with death threats. Her plastic surgeon was there the night she died. Hasn't anybody considered Rob? Your honor, it's almost always the boyfriend. Your honor, did you know she had a penchant for blackmail? Your honor, please pull at any one of these threads. You can pull at any one and find that it wasn't me who did this.*

"This isn't going to work," I whispered to Jack, once he had sat back down next to me. "You have to tell her about Liza. Or Dr. Silver. Or—"

He put a finger to his lips.

"That isn't how this works," he said.

My cheeks were hot but the tears that slid down them then were hotter.

"Please," I said under my breath.

"Mr. Willoughby." Judge Lucas removed her glasses and dangled them impatiently between two fingers. "Is there a problem?"

"No, your honor," he told her, then turned to me and squeezed my hand so tightly I heard a knuckle crack. I couldn't tell if it was his or mine. "Justine," he insisted, looking me dead in the eye, "you need to get it together. You need to take a breath, and you need to let me do my job."

For my wisdom teeth, after an hour of convincing I'd finally let the oral surgeon put me under. He had his technician do it, of course. She'd worn a flamingo-pink gown and matching papery gloves that clung to her wrists with elastic.

"Okay now, sweetie," she said. "I'm gonna have you count down from one hundred, okay?"

Praying for courage, I nodded and started to count. "One hundred, ninety-nine, ninety—" The ceiling lique-fied and went black. Whether I'd wanted to or not, I'd surrendered.

This, I thought, sitting in the courtroom, *this is just like that. You are twelve and you are in the chair and you need to go under now. I'll see you on the other side.*

I felt myself shrink down and slip away like a shadow. Like Peter Pan's shadow when it escapes from him. If I was going to make it through, I'd have to watch this one from the sidelines.

CHAPTER 15

"WITNESS" SLANDERS JUSTINE CHILDS

*J*osie sat up on the witness stand wearing an ankle-length green satin dress and black velvet Mary Janes, her highlighted hair freshly cut into a blunt, shoulder-length bob, her dark eye makeup impeccably feline and winged.

She won't get away with it, I told myself, stroking my own hand beneath the table, feeling the interwoven rise and fall of bone and vein. Somehow the fragility of it was a small comfort.

"Will you please state your name for the court?" the bailiff, a squat man with a Dr. Phil mustache, asked. He waited ceremonially for her reply.

"Josie Bishop," said Josie softly, playing meek.

"Miss Bishop," Melinda Warren greeted her with a tight-lipped smile. "How old are you?"

"Seventeen."

"Are you in school?"

"Yeah. Well, sort of."

"Just a yes or no, Miss Bishop."

"I'm homeschooled. Yes."

"And what grade were you in this past school year?"

"Um . . ." She paused for so long I had to look over at the clock. Almost ten seconds passed before she said, "Eleventh grade."

"During this past July, were you living here in Los Angeles?"

"Yes."

"What neighborhood did you live in?"

"Venice. The canals."

"And what was your address?"

"Eighteen Carroll Canal."

"Who did you live with in July 2018?"

"Eva-Kate Kelly."

"And what was your relationship to Miss Kelly?"

"Uh . . . we'd been friends for many years, and I was working as her personal assistant."

"Did anyone else live with you and Eva-Kate?"

"Yes."

"And who was that?"

"Justine Childs."

"How did you first meet Miss Childs?"

"She came to a party at Eva-Kate's house."

"What were your impressions of her at that time?"

"She was . . ." Josie coughed and sat up straighter. "She was shy and sweet enough, but there was something off about her. I couldn't put my finger on it, but for a while after I just kept thinking *something's not right, something's not right.*"

"Objection," Jack interjected. "Improper opinion."

"Overruled," said Judge Lucas. "I'm allowing it."

"As time went on, did you come to have a better understanding of why you felt that way about her?"

"Yes. I realized she was obsessed with Eva-Kate."

A quiet concerto of murmurs drummed through the crowd.

"Can you explain what you mean by 'obsessed'?"

"Um, yes, sure. She moved into the house and started doing everything Eva-Kate did. She went to all the same parties, she started talking like her and wearing all her clothes. I saw her getting *way* too close with Eva-Kate's ex at a Fourth of July party. It was like she wanted to *be* her. And she was always going into her room late at night, which I thought was kind of creepy and weird. I don't think she knew I could see her sneaking in, but I could. I was always watching, even when she thought I wasn't."

You were always watching me and somehow I'm *the obsessive creep? Maybe* you're *the one obsessed with Eva-Kate,* I thought. *Maybe you couldn't handle that* I *was the one she invited to sleep in her room.*

"And why were you always watching her?"

"Because I didn't trust her. I didn't feel safe with her around. I always had this feeling like I needed to watch my back."

"Now, Miss Bishop, I'd like to direct your attention to the night of July sixteenth. Where were you that night?"

"I was at Eva-Kate's house."

"What time did you arrive there?"

"Around eight at night."

"Where were you coming from?"

"We had been at the Madonna Inn in San Luis Obispo."

"Who is 'we'?"

"Me, Eva-Kate, and Justine. Also Ruby and Zander and Declan."

"Is that Ruby Jones, Zander Linton, and Declan Fischer?"

"Yes."

"And did Ruby, Zander, or Declan return back to Eva-Kate's house after the trip?"

"No."

"Did Justine?"

"Yes. She was in the car with us."

"And what happened when you got home?"

"Um . . . London and Olivia were there. They were upset that we didn't invite them on the trip."

"Is that London Miller and Olivia Law?"

"Yes."

"Why weren't they invited on the trip?"

"Oh . . . I have no idea. That wasn't my call. But by then Eva-Kate and Justine mostly only did things together. Nobody else was invited in those last days."

"But you were invited?"

"To the Madonna Inn, yes. I'm her . . ." She paused. "I *was* her personal assistant. So she took me with her on trips."

"So then Eva-Kate must have trusted you a great deal. A personal assistant has a lot of responsibilities that you don't give to just anybody. She really relied on you."

"Objection." Jack stood. "Your honor, the prosecutor is testifying."

"Sustained. Miss Warren?"

"Of course," Melinda went on without hesitation. "Let's try that again. Josie, can you describe your relationship with Eva-Kate?"

"Yes. We'd known each other for most of our lives. I trusted her with my life, and I'd like to think she trusted me with hers too."

"Okay, so, London and Olivia were frustrated that they didn't get invited. What happened next?"

"Justine went upstairs while Eva-Kate and I stayed downstairs. She asked London and Olivia to leave, because they were being assholes. I mean, sorry! They were, uh . . . I don't know, they were being the spoiled brats they always are."

"Was that the last time you saw Justine that night?"

"No."

"When was the last time you saw Justine that night?"

"About an hour later."

"And what was she doing?"

"She was arguing with Eva-Kate outside Eva-Kate's bedroom. Eva-Kate went outside and Justine followed her."

We weren't arguing. We never argued.

"You say they were arguing. Did you happen to hear what they were arguing about?"

"Justine was angry that Eva-Kate had been keeping a secret from her. Their voices were hushed so I didn't hear the details. Just that there was a secret and Justine was completely flipped out about it."

"I see. And then you say she followed Eva-Kate outside?"

"Yes."

"Did Justine bring anything with her when she went outside?"

"Yes.

"And what was that?"

"The athame."

"For those who don't know, can you tell us what an athame is?"

"It's a dagger used in witchcraft rituals."

"Could you describe what this particular athame looked like?"

"The handle was painted white with blue cornflowers and had a green bow tied around it. The blade was about five inches long."

"No further questions, your honor."

CHAPTER 16

JOSIE BISHOP CROSS-EXAMINED

*T*he self-critic in my mind was on fire and everything I did was wrong. Everything about me was wrong. The way I sat was wrong. First I was too slouched, then I was too poised. I hadn't dressed up nicely enough, then I had dressed too well. I worried the shade of brown I dyed my hair was too dark—*does it make me look devious?* Then I worried I hadn't dyed it dark enough—*why do you always have to go around fixing what isn't broken?*

My cuticles throbbed from where I'd picked at them. My cheek stung where a zit was surfacing, unkind and unforgiving. My ankle muscles ached from standing in heels and the blisters on my heels flared raw.

"Miss Bishop." Jack took Melinda's place standing before Josie. "You knew Eva-Kate for how long?"

"About ten years."

"About ten years," he repeated. "And you're seventeen now. So, that means you met when you were seven?"

"Wow." Josie smirked. "That's some quick math, counselor."

"Answer the question, Miss Bishop," Judge Lucas instructed.

"Yes," she said, uncrossing and recrossing her legs. "We met when we were seven. In school."

"Then this was before Eva-Kate became a big star?"

"Yes. She hadn't even started filming *Jennie* yet."

"Is it true that you're one of her oldest friends? If not *the* oldest?" He paced in front of her, taking one step to the left, two steps to the right, and back again.

"Pretty much."

"Is that a yes?" He took one step closer and looked at her directly until she looked back.

"Yes."

"Would you say you're her *best* friend?"

"I would. Yes."

"At what point did Eva-Kate start paying you to be her friend?"

"Excuse me?"

"Objection," said Melinda. "Argumentative."

"Overruled," said Judge Lucas. "Proceed, Mr. Willoughby."

"You were her *paid assistant*, correct?"

"Yes, but I wasn't *paid to be her friend*. I was paid to help make her life run smoothly."

"I see. Isn't it true that you were living with Eva-Kate at the time of her death?"

"Yes."

"Isn't it true that you were living with Eva-Kate for at least a year before that?"

"Yes . . ."

"Did your parents know that you'd been living at Eva-Kate's?"

"Uh . . ." She glanced nervously at me, then at Melinda. "No . . ."

"Really? How is that possible?"

"They've been living abroad for a few years."

"Interesting. So, then, the *homeschool* you spoke of earlier is really *no school*."

"Uh . . ."

"It's just, if you have no education and nowhere to live, and Eva-Kate was paying you *and* giving you a place to live, it seems you'd be very dependent on her, isn't that so?"

"Sure." Josie rolled her eyes. "Yes."

"Then someone like Justine shows up and is suddenly Eva-Kate's new favorite person, right? She's potentially a threat to your security and cushy setup as Eva-Kate's professional best friend, so you decide you don't trust this new girl, you decide she's suspicious, is that it?"

"She *was* suspicious," Josie insisted. "I didn't just make that up for convenience's sake."

"What about seeing Justine with the athame? Did you make *that* up for convenience's sake?"

"No. I didn't. I saw her take the athame outside."

"You saw her take it all the way outside?"

"Yes."

"Yes?"

"Well, no."

"Which is it, Miss Bishop? Yes or no?"

"I saw her take it and follow Eva-Kate down the stairs."

"But not all the way outside?"

"No."

"I see. I just want to get clear on what you think you did or didn't see."

"I *did* see it."

"And this was on the sixteenth of July?"

"Yes."

"When you'd arrived home from San Luis Obispo?"

"Yes."

"How many alcoholic beverages would you say you'd had the night before?"

"*What?*" Her gaze darted to the judge. "Do I have to answer that?"

"You do." Judge Lucas nodded.

Josie sighed.

"I don't know." She rubbed her temples. "Maybe five?"

"*Maybe five?* Is that a typical amount of drinks for you on any given night, Miss Bishop?"

"No."

"Then you were pretty hungover on that day, the sixteenth of July?"

Josie sighed again. "Yes."

"So, then, isn't there a chance that your hangover and your prejudice against Justine led you to believe you saw something you didn't?"

"I didn't have any prejudice against Justine."

"You didn't? Because we know you had a bad feeling about her, and we know she was threatening your position in Eva-Kate's life. Do you know the definition of prejudice, Miss Bishop?"

"The exact definition? No."

"Great, let me read it for you." He picked a dictionary up off his table and flipped to a bookmarked page and read, "*Preconceived opinion that is not based on reason or actual experience.* Doesn't that sound like your feelings toward Justine?"

"No, because my feelings about Justine were based on reason and experience."

"The experience of seeing Justine spend all her time with Eva-Kate? Because that sounds more like simple jealousy to me."

"Objection, your *honor*," Melinda whined. "Argumentative! Counsel is testifying."

"Try again, Mr. Willoughby," Judge Lucas instructed.

"I wasn't jealous of Justine," Josie cut in before he had a chance to rephrase.

"But you didn't like that she was stealing your best friend?"

"She *wasn't* stealing my best friend."

"But they were doing everything together all the time?"

"Well, yes. But—"

"When you were in San Luis Obispo, is it true that you stayed at the Madonna Inn?"

"Yes . . ."

"And did the three of you share a room?"

"No."

"Is it true that Eva-Kate and Justine shared a room?"

"Yes."

"Then where did *you* sleep?"

"In my own room."

"So they shared a room, and you had to sleep alone."

"I had my own room, but—"

"Miss Bishop," he cut her off. "How is your eyesight?"

"My eyesight?"

"Do you wear glasses? Contacts?"

"Uh . . . yeah . . . I wear glasses at night."

"Are they for reading or for distance?"

"Um . . . distance?"

"So, you need them if you want to see things clearly from a distance at night?"

"Yes."

"On the night of the sixteenth when you think you saw Justine holding the athame, how far away from her were you?"

"I was down the hall. So . . . like, twenty feet."

"And were you wearing your glasses?"

"No." Josie shifted her jaw from side to side. "I wasn't."

"No further questions, your honor."

❈ ❈ ❈

"How did that go?" I asked in the hallway during a recess.

"Fine," he replied, "but it's just getting started."

"*Fine?*" I asked. "What does that mean? Did you prove Josie's an unreliable witness?"

"Prove? No, I didn't *prove*. I showed some evidence that points to her possibly not being reliable. There's not a lot of room for black and white in the American judicial system, but we're building you a defense here, okay?"

"Okay," I said. "Fine." Then I tried hard not to think of spending the rest of my life in a bunk bed with a roommate with a face tattoo and a sadistic streak.

CHAPTER 17

EXHIBIT A FOR ATHAME

*N*ext up was the coroner. Thomas Walker-Flynn. A tall and lanky man, I guessed somewhere in his early sixties, with powdery white eyebrows that loomed crookedly over the rest of his face. His blue silk tie burned against the stark white of his suit jacket.

"Your name, sir?" Melinda Warren asked him, standing with her hands tucked into her blazer pockets, elbows splayed out so that her arms looked like wings.

"Thomas Walker-Flynn." He leaned in to speak into the microphone.

"And who do you work for?"

"LA County Medical Examiner's Office."

"How many years have you worked there, Mr. Walker-Flynn?"

"Almost twenty years."

"What is it that you do at the medical examiner's office?"

"I am a medical examiner. I am charged with examining the bodies of deceased individuals and certifying a cause or manner of death."

"Mr. Walker-Flynn," she went on, "according to your expert opinion, what was the cause of Miss Kelly's death?"

"A knife wound inflicted below her rib cage on the left side. The knife punctured her spleen and severed her thoracic aorta. She bled out extremely quickly and was dead within seconds."

"According to what you found, how big of a blade are we talking about?"

"About five inches. Double-edged."

"So then it was a dagger, and not a knife?"

"That's correct."

"A dagger like this?"

She removed a remote control the size of a business card from her pocket and clicked it in the direction of a projector screen to the left of the room. As she did so, it flickered awake, displaying an image of the athame, the bone-white handle and the double-edged blade rusty with blood. My stomach lurched and my eyes clapped shut.

"Yes, ma'am," he confirmed. "Exactly like that."

"This is People's Exhibit A, your honor," Melinda declared. "The dagger, also known as an athame, that killed Eva-Kate Kelly."

She paused here, opening up a big, blank space I felt myself plunge into.

"According to your findings," she went on, "was this wound inflicted by a large person?"

"Sorry, can you define large?"

"Sure, sure." She bobbed her head. "Six feet or taller?"

"I couldn't say."

"Is it possible for you to tell how tall this person *was*?"

"The dagger went in on a slightly upward angle, which suggests the killer was shorter than the victim."

"*Interesting.*" One side of her mouth twisted up into an amused, sour smirk. "Now, according to your findings, what time did Eva-Kate Kelly die?"

"I can't say a precise time. But it would have been somewhere between midnight and four in the morning."

"Thank you, Mr. Walker-Flynn. No further questions, your honor."

✱ ✱ ✱

"Mr. Walker-Flynn," Jack began, hopping up even before Melinda had finished speaking. "Refresh our memories.

You said Eva-Kate was killed with one stab wound, is that correct?"

"Yes."

"Meaning, she was stabbed one time? Just once?"

"Yes."

"And she died almost immediately?"

"Very quickly, yes."

"Then the killer knew what they were doing?"

"Objection, calls for speculation."

"Sustained."

"Of course." Jack held up a finger, asking for patience. "Let's put it this way: Would an average person know how or be able to end someone's life with one quick stab?"

"Unlikely. It could happen by chance, of course, that someone who had no idea what they were doing got quote unquote *lucky* and inserted the weapon into the exact right spot."

"But most likely an average person would have to inflict multiple wounds, trying at least a few times before cutting into the right spot?"

"Yes. That's right."

"Then, in your expert opinion, is our killer most likely somebody with expertise and knowledge of human anatomy?"

"Most likely, yes."

"*Interesting,*" he shot pointedly in Melinda's direction.

"And you say the time of death was approximately between midnight and four in the morning?"

"Yes, sir."

"But it is possible that the death occurred before midnight or after four? Say, five?"

"It's possible, yes."

"Thank you." He glanced over his shoulder at Melinda to gloat once more. "No further questions, your honor."

✳ ✳ ✳

Judge Lucas had called another recess and I was sitting in a private room with my parents and Jack Willoughby.

"You're doing so good, pumpkin," my dad said. "Phenomenal. Everything's going to be over soon."

No it's not. I wanted to slip away from his hand on my shoulder but sat extremely still. I never knew anymore who was looking. I felt sick to my stomach. My heart thumped deep in my neck tissue like a ticking time bomb hidden away somewhere in the walls. I could feel that the air was cool, but my skin sizzled and my forehead burned with the first signs of a fever. I struggled to swallow. I broke out in a cold sweat.

"I can't do this anymore," I said to Jack, wanting my parents to disappear, wanting the walls and the lights and my bones and my shoes and the chipped tiles they stood on to dissolve, liquefy, and slide off the face of the Earth. "When will it be over?"

"That's extremely hard to say, Justine." He handed me a handkerchief that was white with black polka dots. "There are several witnesses left and—"

"Can you walk us through the rest of the trial?" my mom asked, practically shouting. "I need to know what to expect. I swear I'm on the verge of a heart attack."

"Nancy, breathe." My dad moved his hand from my shoulder to hers, and she slapped it off.

"How can I breathe, Elliot?" Her voice started to tremble. "Do you understand our daughter's life is on the fucking line?"

"Nancy, calm down," he tried again. "Everything is going to be fine. Remember that the worst-case scenario—"

"Mr. Willoughby." She put her hand up to block my dad from her sight. "This isn't going well, I know that, I'm not an idiot. I'm not a lawyer but I'm not a fucking idiot either, so I know shit's going south. They're say-ing my daughter is a crazed stalker killer *freak*, and with her fingerprints on the knife and a witness who says—and all you did in there was a half-assed attempt to prove Josie's unreliable! For what we're paying you, Mr. Willoughby, there has got to be more you can be doing."

"Dr. Childs, Josie *is* an unreliable witness, and the

jury will see that. And getting the coroner to admit that the murder *could* have taken place once Justine was at the hotel is *very* important for us. I'm fairly confident right now that I'll be able to prove that there's simply not enough evidence to convict."

"*That's it?*" My mom clutched at her neck. "That's not enough! Melinda Warren has painted a *very* convincingly lurid image of my daughter, and she *does* have evidence to back it up. She has witnesses. Who cares if they're reliable or not? We don't have any! We don't have anybody on our side!"

"That's not true, Dr. Childs," Jack said. "We have Richie Holmes testifying later, and—"

"Who the hell is that?"

"The man who Justine checked in with at the Ace Hotel. He'll be testifying about the—"

"His testimony is useless! Time of death is approximately between midnight and four in the morning. All he's going to do is testify that she arrived at five; what good is that? Oh God, I can't breathe. Elliot!" She turned back to my dad. "I can't breathe!"

"You can breathe," he said, scratching beneath his chin. "This is just anxiety."

"Dr. Childs, are you all right?" Jack asked her, but looked to me for an answer. I rolled my eyes.

"She doesn't like that the attention isn't on her," I explained. "She's fine."

"Are you kidding me, Justine?" She glowered. "You think anyone would want the kind of attention you've attracted to yourself? You think anyone wants to be a part of this nightmare that you've created?"

"Me?" I laughed. "You're the one who did this! You're the one who led a maniac straight to our door. Now she's dead and the world thinks I killed her. And why? Because *she* was obsessed with *me*. *She* stalked *me*, okay? And you let her. You practically helped her! *None* of this is my fault." I shook my head. "*None.*"

"Okay, okay, okay." Jack Willoughby put his arms out between us, as if he thought we might lunge at each other. "Listen to me, both of you. You're right, the prosecution has painted a picture of Justine as a girl obsessed, but you say if anyone was obsessed, it was Eva-Kate. To the best of your knowledge, is there any evidence that might point to this?"

"My notes," my mom said instantly. "From my sessions with Eva-Kate. They're confidential, but it's all in there—how unstable she was, how fixated she had become. I haven't looked at them lately, but they should illustrate that if anything, Justine is a victim."

"And you'd be willing to submit those?" Jack asked. "Even though it could result in the loss of your license?"

"Of *course*," she said. "This is my daughter's life we're talking about. I'd do anything."

"Okay then." He nodded. "I'll talk to the judge and see what I can do about getting the notes submitted into evidence."

He left us there, and I'd have preferred it if he hadn't, because then I had to look my mom in the eye. And after what she'd just said, I didn't think I could. *She'd do anything for me.* After everything, it was my life that mattered most to her. More than her own. Blood rushed my cheeks, hot and stinging with shame. I hated myself. I had an urge to bash my head into the wall until it was finally all over. I don't know why, but for as long as I can remember, whenever I sense that somebody purely and truly loves me, I want very much to kill myself.

Jack had left the door to our room ajar, and out of the corner of my eye I thought I saw a ghost. A glimmer of blond hair walking by, opalescent skin sculpted into high cheekbones, green-apple eyes. *Liza.* My heart skipped a beat. I watched as she pushed the bathroom door open and went inside.

What's she doing here? I wondered. *After disappearing for months, why show up now?*

To watch you squirm, a voice said. *She wants to watch you take the fall.*

"I need to use the bathroom," I told my parents. "I'll be back in a second."

"What's taking Jack so long?" my mom said, not hearing me. "Where'd he go, anyway?"

"I don't know," I said, keeping my eyes on the bathroom door. "Why don't you go find him. I'll be right back." I hurried down the hall, keeping my head low.

Stop, I told myself, *you look insane. If anyone sees you right now they will think you're insane. If anyone gets a picture of you right now they will think you're insane. Stop walking. Just stop.* But I couldn't stop. I was driven. I took a breath at the bathroom door and pushed it open. Liza stood at the sink applying highlighter to her cheeks. She saw me in the reflection and turned around.

"What do you want?" she asked, capping the highlighter and tossing it into her purse.

"You're letting me take the blame for something you did," I said, trying but failing to keep the tremor out of my voice, "and it's . . . it's not right."

What was I thinking? That she'd confess to me right there in the bathroom?

"Something *I* did?" She gawked. "You must be joking."

"I know Rob's doorman said you were there that night, but you ran away. You left town. With *Rob*. Why would you do that if you didn't have something to hide? It wouldn't be the first time a doorman lied for some cash."

"We didn't leave because we had anything to hide, Justine, we left because our lives here were unmanageable. Do you think we can go *anywhere* in this city without being swarmed? Everywhere Rob goes becomes a circus, and after Eva-Kate died, they started swarming me too. That's no way to live, especially when you're grieving."

"You weren't grieving; you hated her. She took the life that should have been yours and you wanted her dead for it."

"What are you talking about? I told you, I didn't hate her. She hated me."

"You told me they offered you the Jennie role and you turned it down so she could have it. But I don't think that's what happened. I think you wanted it more than anything but they gave it to her. I think you finally got her back when you stole her boyfriend but that still didn't quite feel like enough. Because they chose her, she became a celebrity, she got rich, and what about you? You're just a waitress. You're invisible and it's her fault. So you finally made her pay."

"You sound insane," she said. "And you don't have any proof to back up this little theory."

"Your fingerprints were on the athame," I said. "It could have been you just as much as it could have been me. And whoever hated who, we know your relationship with Eva-Kate was strained. It's all in my mom's notes, and those are being entered into evidence as we speak. She's going to testify to all of it."

"Well, isn't that convenient?" said Liza.

"Isn't what convenient?"

"That it's all in your mom's notes. How supposedly unhealthy our relationship was. It's just very convenient that all of it was documented, don't you think?"

"What are you saying?"

"What I'm saying is that I wouldn't be surprised if the two of you were in it together. She knew she could cover it up by writing these notes that very conveniently draw attention away from herself. Be careful of finger pointers, Justine. It's almost always the finger pointers."

She left me standing alone staring at my own reflection, the bathroom mirror soap-splattered and scratched.

CHAPTER 18

JUSTINE CHILDS PLAYS CAREFREE IN THE RAIN

*I*t rained that night. Dense, heavy sheets of rain plunging, tumbling down my windows. I watched, mesmerized. I love rain. Have I already told you about my love of rain? It makes me feel more at home than home itself. It sounds like a language I knew before birth. It howls renewal and whispers nostalgia. It almost never rains in Los Angeles, but when it does I am guaranteed precious memories.

In fourth grade, for just half the year, I went to the all-girls school Riley was enrolled in. The school was expensive and came with all kinds of perks, my two favorites of which were 1. an environment free of the boys I'd known in public school (absolute terrors), and 2. an adorable uniform composed of a white blouse, red plaid skirt, red cardigan, topped off with a red beret like the maraschino cherry on a sundae. I lived in that outfit. That's what it was to me, not so much a uniform as a second skin that felt so right and so good. Sometimes I even slept in it.

Anyway, one day—a Wednesday, I think—was a day like this, where the rain spills suddenly from the sky, unapologetic and unplanned for. My mom was supposed to pick us up after school, Riley and me. But it was three fifteen and she wasn't there. Then it was four fifteen. Then it was five fifteen and the teachers were all starting to go home and the courtyard lamps were starting to turn off. It was December and so the sun was setting and it was getting dark and the rain was falling harder and harder. Soon the entire campus was empty. After-school care was up and running in the gym, but we weren't enrolled in that, so we huddled underneath one of the classroom awnings, watching rain gush relentlessly from the waterspouts.

At first I panicked. I worried my mom had died in a car crash, skidding across the freeway in the torrential downpour. I worried we'd be kidnapped and then die in a car crash ourselves as the kidnapper attempted to make a quick getaway. I worried we'd drown. I worried we'd survive but have to spend the night sleeping in an abandoned school. I worried we'd have to live there forever, that the storm would wipe out all of civilization and from then on it would just be Riley and me fending for ourselves, feral and rabid, as Saint Catherine of Siena School for Girls crumbled around us. But then Riley dared me to go stand in the rain.

"No way," I said, shuddering in the cold. "You're crazy."

"I'm not crazy," she said. "Are you scared? Are you still a crybaby scaredy-cat?"

"No," I pouted. "I'm not."

I stood there for a minute, feeling my lips turning blue. Then I had the overwhelming need to prove her wrong. To show her I was someone different than who she thought I was. I wanted her to see what I was capable of.

"Fine," I huffed, stomping into the rain. "Are you happy now?"

Water cascaded down my face, rolling off my nose and lips in plump drops.

"Oh my God," she squealed, jumping up and down, "I didn't think you'd do it!"

I could hardly hear her, the rain was so loud in my ears, crashing all around me. To my surprise, I took to it like dried-out soil. My skin drank it up. With each drop I felt more and more alive, more brave, more free. I tilted my face to the sky and let it wash me. I held my arms out and twirled around like Julie Andrews in *The Sound of Music*, feeling like myself, feeling truly Justine for the first time. And, if I really think about it, for the last time. Until the day I met Eva-Kate.

Riley ran out to meet me and we splashed around in the rising puddles, water soaking through our black Velcro Mary Janes, soaking through our tights. We chased each other, giggling, then laughing hysterically, tripping and falling and getting back up to do it all over again until we were wet from head to toe. A mural of Peter Rabbit looked down over us, and I didn't care anymore if anybody ever came for us. In fact, I prayed they wouldn't.

But they did, of course. My mom showed up at five thirty, so apologetic she didn't notice we were drenched. It was Rachel Ames, of course. Again. She'd had several nervous breakdowns since Benji Laramore had left her, and my mother was by her side for every one of them. Riley and I huddled together for warmth in the back seat of the Land Rover, and after we dropped Riley off, my mom helped me out of my uniform and into my favorite pajamas, then wrapped me in a blanket and stroked my hair as I fell asleep to Mary-Kate and Ashley's *Winning London*.

It was one of the many rainy memories I cherished.

That night, after the first day of my trial, I was sure if I could get outside to stand in the rain I could feel okay again, even if just for a moment. But my mom was camped out in an Eames shell chair outside my room, making sure I wouldn't go anywhere. She wasn't wrong to do so. "A Carefree Justine Childs Plays in the Rain After Day in Court" was not a headline that would work in my favor.

My mom took away my Xanax and my alcohol and I had nothing to dull my nerves. I chewed on the inside of my bottom lip until the skin felt like how baked pizza dough feels if you pull the cheese off, tender and blistered. I knocked my hands against the corners of my desk until they bruised and swelled. Pressing on the bruises took my mind off it all. I rubbed my eyes until they stung. I was exhausted but couldn't sleep.

I got on Twitter and tried to numb out. Tried to think of something other than myself. People on Twitter were praying for Notre Dame Cathedral as it burned, laughing—baffled and bemused—at the first ever photograph of a black hole, celebrating Taylor Swift as the video for her latest single, "ME!"—an all fun and games pastel homage to imagination—hit twenty-four-million views in less that twelve hours. Last but not least, the people of Twitter were, it seemed, more or less convinced of my guilt. I was a top four trend.

I smiled. It didn't matter what they were saying about me; this was so fucking cool. I should have left it at that, feeling good for a second. I shouldn't have clicked on the #JustineChilds hashtag, but I had to see.

@TabbyPantano: Justine Childs is sooooooo guilty. She looks legit terrified, cuz she knows what she did.

@AmandaKnoxTruther: She did it! Duh! She was a crazy fan who got unhinged. End of story. Wake up, people.

@SteevieKay: I know she's a killer, but do any other gay boys out there have a taboo crush on Justine Childs?

@CarrieMorseCode: If you think Justine Childs is innocent you are beyond saving.

@MonicaHarmonica: I believe Justine killed Eva-Kate, but I think she is too tiny to have done it alone. I think there were #multiplekillers.

@JayJayVanderoth: Justine is out there playing the victim. Let's not forget the real victim, EVA-KATE KELLY. Justine doesn't seem so sweet after you realize she stabbed that poor girl in cold blood.

"Okay, okay, okay," I said out loud to no one, slamming the computer shut and tossing it out of the way. "I get the picture."

I rolled onto my back and dug my left canine deep into my lip. By that point, the pain didn't even make me flinch. My thoughts kept coming back to Liza and our standoff in the courthouse bathroom.

What I'm saying is that I wouldn't be surprised if the two of you were in it together, she'd said. *She knew she could cover it up by writing these notes that very conveniently draw attention away from herself. Be careful of finger pointers, Justine. It's almost always the finger pointers.*

She was wrong, of course. My mom couldn't have been covering anything up for me, because I didn't do anything, and because I found those notes before Eva-Kate was dead. And, of course, because my mom wasn't even in town yet. Or was she? I didn't want to think about it, but something about Liza's accusation had stuck with me. Was there a way, I had to wonder, that somehow my mom was involved in Eva-Kate's death?

CHAPTER 19

NANCY CHILDS TESTIFIES

*T*he next day in court I was in a painful, sleep-deprived daze. I struggled to keep my eyes open, but my nerves jittered with an ongoing adrenaline spill. I'd let my mom dress me, so I wore a black dress with white pinstripes and my hair clipped to the side with a girlish pink-satin barrette. I had been too weak to put on any makeup, so she hustled concealer and nude lipstick onto me as I slumped against the passenger seat window. It's not that I didn't care anymore; I did. I just didn't have the wherewithal to do anything about it.

A forensics expert, Michael Ferguson, testified for the prosecution that my fingerprints were found on the athame, as well as on multiple glasses in Eva-Kate's bedroom and kitchen. We looked at black-and-white renderings up on a light projector, my fingerprints and the ones found at the crime scene placed side by side, an identical series of looping, swirling ridges, *Under the Wave off Kanagawa* outlined over and over and over. Jack cross-examined and got him to admit that, while my fingerprints were no doubt all over the athame, so were many other people's. Those people included Liza and Debbie McKelvoy. At this, Melinda Warren looked momentarily downcast. Jack turned to give me a wink.

Then the ball was in Jack's court. He called Richie Holmes, the Ace Hotel desk clerk, who testified that I checked in at exactly 5:09 in the morning. Jack reminded the courtroom that it was entirely possible that Eva-Kate had died while I was on my way to the hotel, or even once I had already checked in. From the witness stand, behind horn-rimmed glasses, Richie kept looking over at me. Even when Jack refocused him, his gaze would be back on me in no time. I wondered if it was a compulsive kind of thing. I wondered if he had a crush. He had dark features, brown hair styled back off his forehead, and an elegantly angular nose. I tried to imagine him naked, a pathetic attempt to keep myself from bursting into tears at any second. It didn't work; in the place of a naked body all I saw was amorphous, staticky gray.

Melinda didn't cross-examine, but brought in Douglas

Mathis, the Uber driver who took me to the Ace. His records showed that he picked me up at 4:40. Melinda reminded us all that according to the coroner's report, Eva-Kate most likely died between midnight and four in the morning.

"Forget the time Justine checked into the Ace Hotel," she said. "What matters is that she got into Mr. Mathis's car at four forty. Until that point, her whereabouts are unaccounted for. She has no alibi whatsoever for the window of time in which Eva-Kate died. That part of this case is undisputable."

The room was silent then. I was sure everyone could hear my heart flailing, thumping itself against my chest like a bat in a birdcage.

"We're gonna prove her wrong, don't worry." Jack patted my hand. "Just sit tight."

✳ ✳ ✳

When it was Detective Sato's turn to testify, he climbed up onto the stand with unnerving zest, like this was the moment he'd been waiting for, like this was *his* moment.

"Good afternoon," Melinda said amiably.

"Good afternoon," he replied. His cheeks were slightly sunburned, two red blotches that moved up and down as he spoke.

"Can you please state and spell your name for the court?"

"Detective Trevor Sato. That's Trevor T-R-E-V-O-R Sato S-A-T-O."

"Thank you, Detective. Are you employed currently?"

"Yes."

"Where are you employed?"

"The Los Angeles Police Department. Homicide division."

"What is it that you do in the homicide division?"

"Investigate and aim to solve murders."

"How long have you been a police officer?"

"A little over ten years."

"And how long have you been in your current assignment with the homicide division?"

"Three years."

"Thank you, Detective. Now, I'd like to draw your attention to the afternoon of July seventeenth."

"Yes, ma'am."

"Is this the afternoon you found the body of Eva-Kate Kelly?"

"Yes."

"At what time did you locate the body?"

"1:46 P.M."

"How was it that you came upon the body?"

"We received an anonymous tip. The captain sent Detective John Rayner and myself to investigate the scene at Eighteen Carroll Canal."

"Is it relatively normal to receive an anonymous tip?"

"No, generally not."

"Why would somebody want to report a crime anonymously?"

"Most likely because said person was somehow involved in the crime—or other illegal activity—and is feeling guilty, doesn't want to get caught."

"I see. And what did you discover upon arriving at the scene?"

"A body floating facedown. Half in the water, half washed up onto the shore."

"And this was the body of Eva-Kate Kelly?"

"Yes."

"And were you able to determine cause of death?"

"It was clear that she had been stabbed to death."

"How was that clear?"

"There was a knife sticking out of her. Below her left ribs."

"I see. And what was your role in the investigation of Eva-Kate's death?"

"My role, basically, was to work along with Detective Rayner to determine what happened to Miss Kelly and identify the person responsible."

"To identify who murdered her?"

"Objection. Leading the witness."

"Sustained."

"Allow me to rephrase. During the course of that investigation, did you come to believe that Eva-Kate Kelly was, in fact, murdered?"

"Yes."

"Did you develop a suspect?"

"Yes."

"And who was that suspect?"

"Justine Childs."

"Is that a person you recognize in the courtroom today?"

"Yes."

"Can you please describe where she's seated and what she's wearing?"

"She's sitting in front of me, slightly to my left. She's wearing a dark blue skirt and blazer."

"Thank you. And how did it come to be that Justine was a person of interest?"

"We had an eyewitness inform us that they saw Miss Childs at the scene of the crime holding the murder weapon."

"Was that witness Josie Bishop?"

"Yes."

"Was Miss Bishop's testimony the sole reason you suspected Justine Childs?"

"No. When we tested the knife for fingerprints, it was determined that Justine's were present."

"So, then, it can be concluded that Justine did in fact hold the knife?"

"Objection, your honor." Jack stood. "Argumentative!"

"Sustained."

"Aside from the eyewitness and the fingerprints you found, was there another reason that you came to suspect Miss Childs?"

"The surveillance footage we obtained from Miss Kelly's residence showed Miss Childs following Miss Kelly outside, which corroborated Miss Bishop's testimony."

"Your honor, I'd like to enter into evidence the surveillance tapes from the Kelly residence as Exhibit B. Can we dim the lights?"

The lights dimmed and Melinda guided our attention to the screen. She used her remote to click PLAY. My mom always said so many of her actress patients couldn't stand watching themselves on-screen. She said oftentimes they wouldn't even watch the movies they were in, or, if they did, they'd look away during their scenes. Some, though, would force themselves to watch, knowing it would strengthen their craft if they could study themselves and learn from their mistakes. This was just like that, I told myself. This was just an uncomfortable performance I had to force myself to sit through in order to become stronger.

As the footage played, it showed a black-and-white night-vision version of Eva-Kate and me from a high diagonal angle. It showed us standing near the answering machine, presumably talking, then it showed us walking away down the hall. It wasn't exactly damning evidence of anything. I noted that with my hoodie up, it was hard to fully see my face.

"Detective Sato, can you describe to me, and the jury, what you see in this video?" Melinda asked.

"Miss Childs and Miss Kelly are standing by the telephone in the upstairs hallway at 9:10 P.M. Then they walk away down the hall and Miss Childs follows Miss Kelly down the stairs."

"And does this line up with what your witness Miss Bishop told you?"

"Yes, it does."

"No further questions, your honor."

✳ ✳ ✳

"Detective Sato"—Jack strode out before him—"were Justine's fingerprints the only fingerprints you found on the knife?"

"No."

"Who else's prints were present?"

"Rob Donovan's, Olivia Law's, and Josie Bishop's."

"Then why weren't any of them suspects?"

"There was no witness who saw any of them following Eva-Kate outside with the murder weapon. And none of them were seen on the surveillance footage."

"Well, Josie was seen on the surveillance footage, so we know she was there that night."

"Objection, he's testifying."

"Sustained. Is there a question, Mr. Willoughby?"

"Yes. If Josie was seen on the surveillance footage to be present on the night of Eva-Kate's death, and her fingerprints were found on the weapon, then why was she never considered as a suspect?"

"Well, because she was our main witness, and because the footage corroborated what she said she saw."

"Did it, though? Can we dim the lights and take another look at that footage?"

The lights dimmed and the footage began rolling.

"So," Jack narrated, "here we see Justine and Eva-Kate in the hallway at 9:10 P.M. They seem to be talking. Then they both walk away down the hall." He hit PAUSE as we disappeared down the steps. In the frame on the screen, it looked as if it were actually *Eva-Kate* who was following *me*.

"What we don't see is proof of Miss Bishop's claim that Justine grabbed the athame or that she followed Eva-Kate outside."

"Objection, testifying."

"Sustained. Mr. Willoughby?"

"I apologize, your honor. Detective, in the clip that the prosecution has provided, do we see proof that directly corroborates Miss Bishop's claims?"

"No."

"So, then, considering Josie Bishop was present, isn't it pretty convenient—for her—that she saw Justine carry the athame and follow Eva-Kate outside?"

"Objection." Melinda stood. "Calls for speculation."

"Overruled. Mr. Willoughby, get to your point."

"Yes, your honor. My point is this. Detective, if Josie was present the night of the murder, and her claims that she saw my client with the murder weapon can't actually be backed up, isn't it possible that she killed Eva-Kate?"

"Objection, your honor! Calls for speculation."

"Sustained."

"All right. Let's talk about the time stamp for a second. At what time does Justine supposedly follow Eva-Kate outside?"

"According to the video, 9:11 P.M.," said Detective Sato.

"And yet other records from the night show Eva-Kate still alive at ten, eleven, and twelve o'clock, correct?"

"Yes. Correct."

"And according to the coroner's report, she didn't die until sometime between midnight and four in the morning, correct?"

"Correct."

"So then, if this video doesn't show Justine with the weapon, and it doesn't reflect the point in time when we know Eva-Kate died, isn't it true that it in fact does not show anything of relevance to this case?"

"Objection, testifying!"

"Sustained."

"No further questions, your honor." Jack smiled and sat down. "That's all."

* * *

"Defense, you may call your witness," Judge Lucas instructed.

Jack stood and buttoned his jacket.

"Your honor, the defense calls Dr. Nancy Childs to the stand."

The bailiff let my mom in through a side door, then helped her up onto the witness stand. She wore a linen pantsuit and a pearl necklace I'd never seen before. Her lips were puckered, like she'd just put something sour in her mouth and was considering spitting it out, and her forehead was shiny with sweat that she kept dabbing at with a purple handkerchief.

Her hand trembled lightly as she held it up and swore to tell the truth. The whole truth. I pressed the bruises on my hands to feel something other than completely sick. Sick with fear, sick with shame, sick with the feeling that all of this could have been prevented somehow if only I'd been paying better attention. If only I hadn't been so wrapped up in Eva-Kate's charm, blinded by the lights upon lights upon lights that were her life. I'd forgotten myself entirely. I'd forgotten self-control.

"Dr. Childs," he began, "what is the nature of your relationship to the defendant?"

"She's my daughter."

"Is it true that you also knew Miss Kelly?"

"Yes."

"How did it come to be that you knew Miss Kelly?"

"I was her therapist. From the time she was six or seven."

An intrigued murmur rippled through the crowd of onlookers.

My mom's eyelids flickered. I worried she might faint under the pressure. It wouldn't have been the first time. She fainted when I broke both my collarbones climbing on the frail branches of a dying lemon tree in our backyard when I was five, and she fainted the day the doctors at Bellflower told her that her only daughter was suffering from stress-induced paranoid psychosis.

"Okay, first things first, Dr. Childs." He tapped a pen against the palm of his hand. "Where were you on the night of July sixteenth?"

"I was in Rome," she said. "Getting ready to fly back to Los Angeles."

Was she really? I thought. *Or was she already back by the time she left that voice mail on Eva-Kate's machine?*

And if she was already back, why didn't she come home?
Where was she staying?

I entertained the idea until it almost made sense, twirling it around like a ballerina in my mind, finding that I was enjoying the morbid absurdity of each spin.

"How long were you in Italy?"

"Just a few days. I'd been in India before that."

"When did you first leave the country?"

"At the beginning of the summer. June."

"Did you tell your patient, Eva-Kate Kelly, that you were going away?"

"Yes. She knew I was planning the trip for at least a month before I left."

"How did she respond?"

"Hardly at all." My mom pursed her lips. "She seemed entirely nonplussed. Unaffected."

"So then, she didn't tell you she was planning to buy the house across from yours?"

"Definitely not."

"And yet, she did buy it. Almost as—"

"Objection, counsel is testifying," Melinda complained. "*Again.*"

"I apologize, your honor. Dr. Childs, did Eva-Kate Kelly buy the house across from yours on Carroll Canal?"

"Yes."

"And is it true that she did so while your

daughter, Justine, was spending the summer alone, unsupervised?"

"Justine was supposed to be staying with her aunt, actually. But I didn't tell Eva-Kate that, so . . ."

"Do you have any idea why Eva-Kate might have done this? And without telling you of her plans?"

"Eva-Kate had developed a fixation with my family. Specifically with my daughter, Justine. Over the years, she had grown more and more interested, asking more and more questions, always as if trying to get to know Justine. She had this idea in her head that Justine had a normal, grounded life, and that therefore Justine was more real than she herself was. The idea worked its way into an obsession when her longtime boyfriend, Rob Donovan, broke things off with her."

"An obsession?" Jack asked rhetorically. "That's interesting. So, then, would it be safe to say it was an obsession that drove Eva-Kate to buy a house directly across from where your daughter was living?"

"I believe so, yes. She obviously didn't tell me about her plan because I would have tried to stop it."

"Then is it also safe to say Eva-Kate knew about your daughter long before your daughter knew about her?"

"Yes. I mean, maybe Justine knew Eva-Kate from TV, but so did most of America."

"Right, right. I just think it's interesting how the prosecution is accusing Justine of having some unhealthy obsession with Eva-Kate, when Eva-Kate was actually the one who spent four point five million dollars to live across from Justine."

"Objection, your honor." Melinda shot up, indignant.

"Withdrawn." Jack held up his hands in surrender. "I'll move on. Dr. Childs, do you know what this is?"

He held up a glossy photograph for her to see. She put on a pair of acrylic-frame glasses and squinted performatively. Of course she knew, and I knew too. It was the locked file cabinet where she kept her patient notes.

"Yes," she said. "That's my file cabinet."

Jack rotated the photo slightly so that it faced Judge Lucas, then set it down on the table in front of me.

"Your honor, I'd like to enter Nancy Child's file cabinet as Defense Exhibit One."

"Noted." Judge Lucas nodded.

"And what did you keep in this file cabinet?"

"Notes that I took during my sessions with patients."

"Confidential notes?"

"Yes."

"Then is it safe to say this file cabinet has a secure lock system?"

"Yes." She nodded. "As you can see, it has a keypad on it. You have to type in the code to gain access. It makes a record of every time it's opened."

"So, every time someone unlocks it, a record is made within the device? It keeps track of the times it's been opened?"

"Yep."

"Sorry, Dr. Childs, is that a yes?"

"Yes."

"Your honor, in addition to the file cabinet, I'd like to enter these photocopies of the digital logs tracked by the file cabinet as Defense Exhibit Two. And if it pleases the court, I'd like to review a portion of the transcript."

"Objection, your honor." Melinda stiffened like an arrow. "Relevance?"

"I'm getting to it," Jack promised. "And it's highly relevant."

"Overruled," Judge Lucas proclaimed, leaving Melinda with a resentful pout. "But get there soon, Mr. Willoughby."

"Kazuo King Locks and Security," he resumed, reading off the page. "Login records. Dr. Nancy Childs, PhD. June 2018."

He paused, inspired, perhaps, and handed the page to my mom, who looked bewildered and pale as a sheet.

"Dr. Childs, can you read me the last entry that was documented in June?"

"Sure." She squinted again through her glasses. "It says . . . June twenty-fifth. In, 3:04 P.M., out, 3:45 P.M."

"Thank you, Dr. Childs. Can you tell the court what that means to you?"

"It means I unlocked the files at 3:04, spent about forty minutes writing notes, then locked them back up at 3:45."

"Lovely," he said. "Now can you read me the first entry for July?"

He walked to her and slid his finger down the page, then pointed at it with a flourish, jamming his finger down so it made an audible pop. I cringed, thinking of the bone crunching up somewhere inside his flesh.

"Uh . . ." She scanned for it. "Right. Here, um, July sixteenth. In, 10:00 P.M., out, 4:22 A.M."

"Was that you who unlocked the files at 10:00 P.M. on July sixteenth?"

"No. As I previously testified, I wasn't back in the country yet."

"Then who was it?"

"It would have to have been Justine. Nobody else has keys to our home."

"Not even Mr. Childs?"

"He moved out. I changed the locks."

"So then, according to this Kazuo King lock system, Justine was, in fact, in your home from 10:00 P.M. to 4:22 A.M., the window of time during which Eva-Kate was killed."

"Objection." Melinda held up her hand. "Calls for speculation."

"Sustained."

"No further questions, your honor."

Thanks to that elegant unfolding of information, I experienced a few moments of glorious relief, a light twinkling quietly at the end of the tunnel, a pretty little hope that it all might actually turn out okay. Then Melinda spoke.

"Dr. Childs, you were Eva-Kate's therapist, is that correct?"

"Yes. That's correct."

"A licensed therapist is required to keep patient records confidential, is that right?"

"Yes."

"And does that expectation of confidentiality survive the death of a patient?"

"Traditionally it does, yes."

"And yet you're willing to testify here today about Miss Kelly's therapy, potentially breaching confidentiality?"

"I am."

"In spite of the legal and professional consequences that could result for you personally?"

"Yes."

"And by testifying today, you're breaking patient-doctor confidentiality?"

"Yes."

"Which is against your ethical obligation and may result in the loss of your license to practice?"

"Yes."

"Then it's safe to say you're willing to do quite a lot to protect your daughter?"

"As would most mothers, yes."

"If you're willing to lose your license to protect your daughter, then you'd most likely be willing to lie under oath for your daughter, isn't that correct?"

"No," my mom protested. "Of course not. I wouldn't. I respect the law. And the court."

"It's interesting that your supposed respect for the law and the court doesn't extend to patient confidentiality."

"Objection," Jack interjected. "Argumentative."

"I'll allow it," said the judge.

"How can we know when your unique moral compass urges you to follow the rules or allows you to break them? If you're willing to break the rule of patient confidentiality to save your daughter, how do we know you aren't willing to break the 'whole truth and nothing but the truth' rule in court?"

"I . . . I'm . . ." My mom was turning red. "There's no way for us to ever truly know what somebody is capable of. Someone you might think is purely honest with no special interests could sit up here and lie through their teeth, and you might never know the difference. Then there's me. I may have conflicts of interest, and you might not believe that I'm here to tell the truth, but I am. But no, District Attorney Warren, there's no way for me to convince you of that."

"I see." Melinda kneaded the side of her neck with two fingers. "Is it true that a lot of your clients are celebrities?"

"Some are," she said. "Not all."

"Would you say the majority?"

"I'd say about half."

"And Justine has been aware of this throughout her life?"

"Aside from one patient who consented to meeting Justine many years ago, there'd be no way for Justine to learn the identities of my patients."

"This was not Eva-Kate, but another patient?"

"Yes."

"So then Justine has learned the identities of at least two of your patients."

"There were extenuating circumstances in both cases, but yes."

"Though you claim these are the only two celebrity patients Justine was made aware of, did she know that half the people you treat are celebrities?"

"It's possible that she was aware, yes."

"And are you a dedicated therapist, would you say? Are you good at your job? Do you go the extra mile?"

"Of course."

"So, if you were with your daughter and an incident arose with one of your celebrity patients that required your attention, would you leave your daughter to attend to said situation?"

"If she were being left in a safe situation such as in the care of her father or babysitter, sure. Yes."

"In your professional opinion, what kind of effect do you think that would have on her psyche?"

"Objection. Relevance?"

"Your honor, it speaks to Miss Child's mental state as it pertains to her relationship with Miss Kelly."

"Overruled. Dr. Childs, you can answer."

"I don't think I understand the question."

"To have her mother paying such close attention to celebrities, instead of to her—what emotional toll would that take on her psyche? Wouldn't it lead to feelings of inferiority and possibly resentment toward celebrities?"

"I wouldn't say I paid more attention to my patients than to my daughter. I've been a highly devoted mother."

"As she was growing up, did you pick her up from school?"

"No, normally not."

"Why not?"

"Schools get out around three. That's the middle of the day. I had to work."

"You had to be with patients instead of picking your daughter up from school."

"It's not unusual to be a working parent. Not everyone can just sit around all day twirling their thumbs while they wait for school to let out."

"I'm not accusing you of being neglectful, I'm only saying the specifics of your situation are one that could breed feelings of inferiority or an unhealthy relationship to celebrities, don't you think?"

"Sure, I guess that's . . . possible."

"Let's revisit that fancy file cabinet you have."

"Sure."

"You say there's a mechanism that tracks when the cabinet is unlocked and relocked, is that right?"

"Yes."

"And according to the records from the night of July sixteenth, the cabinet was unlocked between 11:00 P.M. and 4:22 A.M.?"

"Yes."

"Does this 'tracker' system come with a camera?"

"A camera? No . . ."

"So then, we don't have any evidence that it was Justine who unlocked the cabinet and not somebody else?"

"No, but—"

"All we have is proof that somebody was there to unlock the cabinet at 11:00 P.M., but no proof that it was your daughter, Justine?"

"There's no camera, but I'm sure you'd find her fingerprints there if you checked."

"Right." Melinda smiled. "She's lived there her whole life so I'm *sure* we'd find her fingerprints. But is there a way to prove her fingerprints were there from that night? Do her fingerprints prove that she was the one to open the file cabinet that night?"

"She'd never opened it before that night."

"And you're sure about that?"

"Well." My mom deflated. "I can't be entirely sure. No."

"No further questions, your honor."

CHAPTER 20

JUSTINE CHILDS—HAS SHE LOST HER MIND?

"*I*t's like a chess game from hell," I said to Jack, clutching my stomach back in our private room. "We're just going to go back and forth like this forever, nobody really proving anything, and it's going to kill me. I can't stay calm for too much longer."

I bit a piece of dry skin on my thumb and ripped it off. My insides felt scooped out, like a pumpkin on Halloween. I thought of how we used to carve a jack-o'-lantern, pulling the pumpkin guts out with our bare hands, for what felt like hours, until it was finally empty. I saw myself as that pumpkin, gutless, eyes cut out in crooked triangles, jagged candlelight shining through.

"It's good, Justine," he told me. "It means there's not enough evidence either way."

"Okay, so, what, it's like a tie?" I knew how ridiculous I sounded.

"Well, no . . . the jury is still going to have to find you guilty or not guilty. And then the judge will enter her judgment on the verdict."

Guilty. Judgment. The words swarmed in my stomach, buzzing and acidic.

"I don't have a good feeling about this." I tried not to whine, but the words came out frantic and entitled anyway. "The judge thinks I'm a sociopath, I can tell. I can tell she doesn't like me. Right? It's bad. Is it bad? It's bad, isn't it? I can't tell. What's going to happen?"

"First of all, breathe." He put his palms on my triceps. "This is almost over, and whatever the verdict, we will get you through this. I sincerely urge you to—"

"I have to testify," I said then, cutting him off. In the tornado of my thoughts, this was one I could grab on to. "They have to hear my side of the story."

"No, no," he insisted. "That's my job, not yours. That's literally why I'm here, Justine, to tell your side of the story. To defend you."

"I don't know, I don't know." I ran my hands through my hair. "They need to hear it from me. How can anyone really believe in my innocence if they don't hear me claim it?"

"Justine, listen. It's not a good idea."

"You can't stop me, can you? Isn't it my right or something?"

❋ ❋ ❋

The witness stand wasn't all that high up, but I felt wildly, fantastically elevated. The audience watching me down below seemed very far away, their faces blurred and blank. A wave of dizziness swept over me and I tried to remember when I'd last eaten, but it wasn't easy. The day before, my mom had brought toast and jam to me in bed. I'd nibbled at the flaky crust, then the strawberry-logged bread, forcing myself to swallow bite after bite until it was all gone. It had taken me an hour to get it all down. My stomach was like a clenched rubber fist.

"Miss Childs, will you please spell your name for the court?" Jack asked. He faced me, a safe distance of five feet between us.

"J-U-S . . . T-I-N . . . E," I wavered, wiping my fore-head with the back of my palm. "C-H . . . I-L-D-S."

"Thank you, Miss Childs. How was it that you came to meet Eva-Kate Kelly?"

"I, uh . . . she, she moved into the house across from where I live."

"Is that the house you've lived in with your mother and father since you were a child?"

"For my whole life, yes."

"I \see. And when you first met Eva-Kate, did you know that she was a patient of your mother's?"

"No. I had no idea."

"And she didn't tell you?"

"She didn't tell me," I repeated.

"So, then, she probably didn't tell you that she didn't only know your mom, but she also knew you?"

"No, she didn't. I mean, she didn't tell me."

"But you found out later on that in fact she had known your mother and known of you for many years, is that right?"

"Yes. That's right."

"How would you describe the nature of your friend-ship with Eva-Kate as it unfolded over the course of the summer?"

"Um . . . it was fast. She was extremely nice to me right away. I was surprised by how welcoming she was. I felt, or, I mean, it *seemed* like we just connected. We just started hanging out all the time. She invited me everywhere."

"At what point did she invite you to move in to her home?"

"Uh, well . . . I think just two days after we met."

"Did you ever think—and I mean no offense whatsoever—that it was odd for somebody as rich and famous as Eva-Kate Kelly to be taking an interest in someone who, by all appearances, is just an average girl next door?"

I knew what he was doing but it stung anyway. Even knowing, as I did now, that Eva-Kate Kelly was jealous of me, I still wanted the world to look at me and see her equal.

"I did." I told the truth. "I wondered about it all the time. I wondered *why me?* It never made sense."

"Until you found out through your mother's notes that Eva-Kate had been watching you for years."

"Objection. Testifying."

"Sustained."

"Apologies," Jack said. "Justine, did Eva-Kate's interest in you make sense once you read your mother's notes?"

"Yes. It made a bit more sense then. I still don't understand it completely, but I don't think I ever will. Especially with Eva-Kate not around to explain it. What she saw in me, I mean."

"Let's talk about the night Eva-Kate died." He took a few steps back and pressed his fingers together until his hands formed a diamond shape. "Did you see her that night?"

"Yes. We came back from San Luis Obispo around nine. I was with her."

"What happened then?"

"I went upstairs soon after we got home and I heard a voice mail being left on her landline."

"And what did you hear on the voice message?"

"It was my mom . . . calling to schedule an appointment with her. With Eva-Kate."

"But, up until that point, you didn't know that Eva-Kate was a patient of your mother's?"

"Yes. That's right. I didn't know."

"How did that make you feel?"

"Um . . . kind of creeped out? It was like this thing was hiding in plain sight but I never saw it. It's spooky, you know, when you can't see what's sitting right in front of you. I kept thinking I should have known, and I kept wondering why she didn't tell me."

"Okay, so, what did you do?"

"I confronted her about it and she shrugged it off like it was nothing. She, uh, she said she'd told my mom that she was planning to buy the house, but that seemed like a lie to me."

"What made it seem like a lie?"

"My mom is, well, she has been really protective of me for as long as I can remember. She's never wanted me to get into trouble. And if she was Eva-Kate's therapist, then she knew about her party girl reputation, right? So if she had really known Eva-Kate was moving in, she wouldn't have left without warning me to stay away from her."

"I see. What did you do next?"

"I didn't feel safe there anymore. I didn't trust her

and felt like something bad would happen if I stayed. So I went home. That had to be around nine thirty or ten."

"Okay, so, you went home. You found your mom's notes outlining her many years of work with Eva-Kate. How long were you at home going over these notes?"

"Hours," I said. "I stayed there until early morning, when I decided to go to a hotel."

"Did you leave your home at any point?"

"No. Not until I left for the Ace."

"Which, according to your Uber driver's testimony, was at four forty in the morning."

"Right."

"So, from approximately nine thirty at night to four thirty in the morning, you were at home?"

"Yes, that's correct. I had like eight years of notes to go through. And they were enthralling, to say the least."

"How did you get into the cabinet? Wasn't it locked?"

"It was locked, but I guessed the code."

"And what was the code?"

"Uh . . . it was 061300."

"Did those numbers mean anything to you?"

"Yeah. Yes. It's Eva-Kate's birthday."

"Did you think it was strange that your mother

would use Eva-Kate's birthday as the code to her locked cabinets?"

"Uh . . ." I hadn't been expecting him to ask me this, so I stumbled. What was he getting at? Was he trying to cast suspicion on my mom? "Yes, I thought it was kind of strange."

"Thank you, Justine. I only have one more question. How did your fingerprints end up on the athame?"

"One night, I was with Eva-Kate and she showed it to me. She told me to hold it. She said that holding it would feel empowering."

"And *did* it feel empowering?"

"No," I lied. "It didn't feel particularly special. It didn't really feel like anything."

"No further questions, your honor."

* * *

"Hi, Justine." Melinda stood up and buttoned her blue blazer so that it cinched her already slender waist. "How are you doing?"

"Um . . . not ideal, but I'm . . . fine. Thanks."

"Good," she chirped, uncharacteristically upbeat. "According to your testimony, Eva-Kate knew you before you knew her, but didn't tell you. Is that right?"

"Yes."

"When you met Eva-Kate, isn't it true that you also knew who she was, but didn't tell her?"

"Yes, but that's different. She's a celebrity. Everyone knows her."

"But you knew who she was and acted as if you didn't?"

"Sure. Yes."

"And yet you claim you were disturbed to learn that she had done the same exact thing?"

"Again, it's *not* the same thing."

"Your testimony, as well as your mother's, paints Eva-Kate as a girl obsessed. She hunted you down, picked you out, stalked you. According to the way you put it, she was unstable, and you were just a 'regular girl' she fixated on, is that correct?"

"It does seem unstable to me to go so far as to buy a home across from mine."

"Interesting. Are *you* stable?"

"Excuse me?"

"You have a history of mental health issues, isn't that right?"

"Uh." I felt my throat start to tighten and my heart speed up in response. "I guess."

"Is that a yes or a no?"

I swallowed again and again, trying to loosen the tubing, but it was as if a piece of bread were lodged inside, expanding.

"Yes," I managed to get out. I dug a fingernail deep into my thigh once and then again on an angle to make an X.

"Isn't it true that in 2015 you were committed for three weeks to the Bellflower Psychiatric Hospital in Long Beach?"

"Yes."

"And the Bellflower Psychiatric Hospital is an institution for patients suffering from severe psychosis, is that correct?"

"I guess."

"Is that a yes or a no, Miss Childs?"

"Yes."

"Are you aware that in order to be committed to Bellflower you have to be considered a danger to yourself or others?"

"Sure. Yes."

"So which were you?"

"Excuse me?"

"The night your parents had you committed, were you considered a danger to yourself or to others? Or both?"

"Myself," I said. "Never in my life have I been a danger to others."

"I see. Is it true you had a knife and were planning to commit suicide?"

"Yes, but I wasn't—"

"You weren't in your right mind, were you?"

"No, I wasn't."

"Objection, your honor, relevance?" Jack tried.

"Your honor, this information is highly relevant. It speaks to whether or not Justine Childs could have entered an altered mental state in which she felt it acceptable to commit murder."

"I'll allow it; continue," Judge Lucas said.

"Is it true that you were having the psychotic delusion that"—she paused to read off a piece of paper—"you were the physical manifestation of evil and that the sun would never rise again unless you removed yourself from the planet?"

"Yeah . . . yes. How do you know that?" She ignored my question, and I guessed my mom wasn't the only one sharing confidential medical records.

"So then, it's safe to say you have had your share of instability in this life, yes?"

"Sure. Yes."

"Let's jump ahead a few years to this past summer, the summer of 2018, on the night of July sixteenth. How stable were you that night?"

"Uh . . . I was stable. It's been three years since my incident and I've been on regulated medications since then."

"Is it true that the previous night you had been drinking and ended up staying awake until morning?"

"Pretty much . . ."

"And these medications you're on, they don't mix well with alcohol, do they?"

"No." I cringed. "No, they don't."

"But you chose to drink on these medications anyway, is that correct?"

"Yes."

"That doesn't sound like a very stable decision to me; does it to you?"

"No, but—"

"So, with your history of mental illness and the poor decision to mix medication with alcohol, you went back to Eva-Kate's house that night and found out that, for years, Eva-Kate had been going to see your mom for therapy and nobody had told you. That made you feel betrayed, didn't it?"

"Actually, yes."

"So then you confronted her about it, is that right?"

"Yes."

"And is that when you decided to kill Eva-Kate?"

"Are you kidding me?" I gawked. "Absolutely not."

"A witness, Josie Bishop, saw you take the athame and follow Eva-Kate outside, so did you plan to kill Eva-Kate or did you just snap in a moment of rage?"

"Neither! I didn't . . . what Josie says she saw . . . that didn't happen." I struggled, my tongue feeling thick and limp. "I didn't take the knife, I didn't kill Eva-Kate. I went home."

"So you say. And yet, there's nobody to corroborate this story."

"That's not true," I said. "The locked files recorded me using them until after four in the morning."

"No, not quite." DA Warren tilted her head, cutely feigning curiosity. "As I established earlier, the files recorded *somebody* opening them, but they didn't record *you*."

"It *was* me."

"Are you sure?"

"Of course I am."

"Like the time you were sure we'd never live to see another sunrise unless you ended your own life?"

"This is completely different! I was . . . I was experiencing psychosis when . . . when I thought that about myself. I hadn't slept in days, I wasn't in my right mind."

"Didn't you just testify, Justine, that on the night of Eva-Kate's death, you had been sleep deprived, drinking, and taking medications incompatible with alcohol?"

"Yes, but—"

"So, then, isn't it possible that your version of where you were or what you did that night might not be the most . . . *reliable*?"

"But I—"

"Isn't it possible that you, in fact, slipped right back into a state of psychosis that night and out of fear, or jealousy, or some combination of both, decided Eva-Kate had to die?"

"No." I glowered, cheeks hot, heart pumping in my throat so hard it made my jawbone rattle. "It's not."

"No further questions, your honor."

CHAPTER 21

A VERDICT FOR JUSTINE CHILDS

*O*n the day of closing arguments, Judge Victoria Lucas wore her stringy strawberry-blond hair in a bun, and a pink silk scarf tied around her neck. It was still raining, and I hoped it would never stop. For the first time in months I'd slept peacefully through the night. I didn't know if I'd go free or spend years behind bars, but I knew that soon the anticipation would be over and I could start to put this behind me.

"Eva-Kate Kelly was a celebrity," Melinda Warren began, rising from her desk like an effigy. "But she was also a teenage girl. Evelyn Kathleen McKelvoy liked spending time with her friends, watching movies, swimming, traveling. She had a mother, a stepfather, and a twin sister who loved her very much. But she won't be spending any more time with her friends, and her family won't get to tell her they love her ever again. Because she's dead. She's dead through no fault of her own. She's dead because a girl named Justine Childs had a twisted obsession and a wild jealous streak that she couldn't keep under control. She is dead because Justine Childs decided she shouldn't be alive anymore. She's dead because on the night of July sixteenth, 2018, Justine Childs found out that her own mother had been seeing Eva-Kate as a therapy patient and that neither of them had ever told her. See, Justine's mother, Nancy Childs, is a therapist to the stars. Justine was raised glorifying celebrity, seeing time and time again how her mother gave celebrities her undivided attention, something Justine herself couldn't seem to get. Justine's new best friend, Eva-Kate Kelly, had everything Justine wanted and always had to live without—money, beauty, fame— so, when she learned that on top of everything else, Eva-Kate had her own mother's attention, the attention she believed she deserved, she lost it. Eva-Kate Kelly is dead because in that moment, Justine Childs hatched a plan. She is dead because Justine followed through on that plan, taking the athame from the bedroom and asking to talk to Eva-Kate outside. She's dead because some time between midnight on July the sixteenth and 4:00 A.M. on July the seventeenth, Justine used that athame to stab her to death. Justine wants you to believe that she was at her mother's house during that time, but she can't prove it. No witnesses, no proof, only her word. What we do have is her fingerprints on the murder weapon, an eyewitness, and a history of being considered a harm to herself and/or others. Justine Childs has composed herself for court; she's dressed conservatively, smiled politely, and told you a well-crafted story in which *she* is the victim. Do not be fooled. Justine Childs is not a sweet girl, she is a killer, and should be convicted as such."

How is she so sure I'm guilty? I wondered. If she really thought of me as a murderer, would she be afraid to meet me alone at night in a dark alley? Little old me? It was a ridiculous thought, that anybody at all could be afraid of someone as insignificant as I am. But I felt a little bit powerful just knowing it was possible.

"We've heard closing arguments from the prosecution," said Judge Lucas. "Is the defense ready to deliver their closing argument?"

"Yes, your honor." Jack stood up behind me, resting his hands on the back of my chair, and hovered there for a moment. Then he crossed in front of the table so that he was face-to-face with Judge Lucas. "This is a case," he went on, "about friendship, fascination, and even obsession. It is unclear, however, who was the obsessed, and who was the object of that obsession. It is clear that Eva-Kate Kelly and Justine Childs had an intense relationship. It is unclear, however, why Justine would ever want to hurt Eva-Kate in any way whatsoever. Furthermore, there is no evidence to prove that she did! There is no evidence to prove, as Miss Warren claims, that Justine was obsessed with Eva-Kate. In fact, there is evidence that Eva-Kate was the one obsessed with Justine for many, many years. There is no evidence to back Miss Warren's theory that Justine was painfully jealous of Eva-Kate. Miss Warren says that Eva-Kate had everything Justine always had to live without—money, beauty, fame— but my client is beautiful in her own right, and always has been. The Childs family may not be celebrity-level wealthy, they may not have a private jet or drive luxury cars, but they are in no way deprived. Here in Los Angeles, California, extreme wealth is very visible. We see excessive and even obscene levels of money being flaunted everywhere we look. Naturally plenty of people fantasize about what such a surreal and seemingly supernatural life would be like, but celebrity lifestyle envy is hardly a motive for murder. To claim so would be absolutely absurd. We all live in Los Angeles too, don't we? Have any of us contemplated killing a neighbor simply because they might be richer or more famous?" Jack laughed at the idea, giving the jury a moment to do so as well. "I don't think so. Furthermore, with Eva-Kate's help, Justine had started making her own money, and in the short amount of time the two were friends, Justine's Instagram following grew from thirty-five people to over a hundred thousand. Eva-Kate didn't hold Justine back from achieving fame or from making money; in fact, she led her right to it! Why would Justine want to harm somebody who helped her get the very things she'd always wanted? Doesn't make sense, does it? There were, however, other people in Eva-Kate's life who would want to harm her. Miss Warren says that Eva-Kate had friends and family who loved her very much, but, sadly, that wasn't the case. She was emancipated from her parents, who a court deemed unfit to raise her, estranged from her sister after a huge betrayal, and never felt that she could trust her friends. There were many people who had their reasons for wanting to hurt Eva-Kate, including her friends and family members. Her ex-boyfriend, her scorned assistant, even her own mother, just to name a few—but Justine Childs was not one of them. Your honor, ladies and gentlemen of the jury, the evidence to convict my client does not exist. Justine didn't have to testify, but she wanted to tell her story. She thought it was important to tell the court what happened, and she did so with grace and dignity. It's the prosecution's job to prove the charges beyond a reasonable doubt, but that has not been done. Not even close. To convict Justine Childs would be to convict a truly innocent young woman and unnecessarily, unjustly ruin her otherwise bright future. It is my belief that anyone who has heard the evidence must understand this to be the truth."

"Thank you to the prosecution and to the defense," said Judge Lucas. "The bailiff will now take charge of the jurors. The jurors may deliberate until 4:30 P.M. If a verdict hasn't been reached, deliberations will continue tomorrow at 9:00 A.M."

✖ ✖ ✖

Jack said this part could take a while, and that we should go home. My dad came over and brought vanilla ice cream cups with chocolate fudge, the kind you scoop with a flat wooden spoon. My mom put one of the cups in front of me and said, "Eat, Justine, you have to eat something." So I took the spoon out of its paper wrapping and chewed on it until it was soggy and splintered. I liked the taste of wood. *If they lock me up*, I thought, *I'll chew on wooden spoons until I waste away. If they can't see me, I won't really be there.*

"Do you want to watch a movie?" my mom asked. "I can put *Bye Bye Birdie* on in the bedroom and we can lie down."

"*Bye Bye Birdie*?" I asked. Keeping my head upright was becoming a tremendous chore. "Why?"

"It's your favorite. And it's so fun. Come on, we'll take our mind off things just for a bit."

"*Bye Bye Birdie* hasn't been my favorite movie since I was like seven," I said. "I just want to go to sleep."

"You shouldn't sleep yet," my dad said. "The jury could come back with a verdict any minute."

"Oh, I don't know about that," said my mom, swallowing a Xanax with Perrier. "I think this could take a while. Doubt we'll be hearing until tomorrow."

"Hey," my dad said, spotting the near-empty cabinet. "Didn't I have some liquor here? Where'd it go?"

"I drank it," I said, and went to my room. When you've been accused of murder, you can't get in much trouble for swiping a bit of your dad's liquor, now can you?

In my room I started *Donnie Darko* from the beginning and wondered how I'd ever be able to be the same again once the trial was over. Whatever the verdict, would I ever be okay again? In "All Too Well" when Taylor Swift says, "I'd like to be my old self again, but I'm still trying to find it," she's talking about trauma. When you experience trauma, you lose yourself and your sense of reality. The song is about relocating your lost self and recentering yourself in what is real. Which implies, of course, that dating Jake Gyllenhaal was a trauma. He's the exact combination of handsome and irrevocably weird that I could see wreaking psychological havoc on the female mind. I found myself wanting to know him.

As it turned out, neither of my parents was right. It was more than minutes and sooner than tomorrow. It was two and a half hours before we were called back to court.

"This seems like it happened really fast," my mom said in the car. "I don't like this, Elliot. They're going to find her guilty, aren't they?"

"We have no way of knowing. We have to prepare for all possible outcomes."

"I'm not preparing for my daughter to go to prison, Elliot."

"We have to be realistic."

"We could leave," she said then. "We could go to South America. I know someone with a plane, I could call—"

"Your ex-boyfriend the drug smuggler? No, Nancy, you're not doing that."

"If they find her guilty, they'll send her to jail, Elliot, probably for a very long time. I can't let that happen. We need to get out of here."

"You need to calm down," my dad said. "Pull over."

Reluctantly, my mom pulled over and let him take the wheel. She sat in the passenger seat, sweaty and pale. I closed my eyes and told myself I'd be okay in prison.

I'd make friends, I'd write my memoir and sell a million copies. There'd be a TV show. I'd be remembered. It was a nice story, a lullaby I'd sing myself to sleep with every night, if it came down to that.

The cameras followed us up to the courthouse, reporters biting out their questions. Was I looking forward to all of this being over, they wanted to know. What did I think it meant that the jury had come to such a quick decision, they wanted to know. But, most of all, Justine, did you do it? They wanted to know.

In the lobby, a guard scanned me head to toe with a metal detector and I saw I was being filmed through the window. Unable to resist, I smiled at the camera.

"Feeling pretty confident about the verdict, are we?" Melinda said, strolling through the stationary metal detector.

"Not especially," I told her, wiping the smile off my face.

"I wouldn't be if I were you," she said, lifting her watch from the tray and securing it back around her wrist. "If I were you I'd prepare for the worst."

✳ ✳ ✳

Back in the courtroom, sweating, I took my blazer off. Then I was freezing, shivering, goose bumps ravaging my arms, so I put it back on and rubbed my hands together. I imagined I could rub them so hard and so fast they'd catch fire and I'd go up in flames. That, I thought, would be better than the waiting.

"All rise for the honorable Judge Lucas," the bailiff boomed. We rose, the shuffling of feet and chair legs filling the room, and Judge Lucas climbed up onto her bench.

"Thank you all for returning so promptly. I *am* somewhat surprised at how quickly we're finding ourselves back here, but I trust the jury took all the facts into consideration and used their greatest judgment in deliberation. So, folks"—she turned to the jury—"have you reached a verdict?"

"We have, your honor." The foreman stood.

"Will the defendant rise," Judge Victoria Lucas said. A command, not a request.

I stood up, knees quaking.

"You may proceed, Mr. Foreman," she told him.

"On the count of murder in the second degree, we find the defendant, Justine Childs . . ."

CHAPTER 22

JUSTINE CHILDS, THE VERDICT PART 2

"*N*ot guilty."

My knees buckled and I fell to the chair. I cupped my face in my hands and stared dumbly in disbelief. A wall of sound erupted all around me, everything slow and surreal and safe.

"Justine." I could hear Jack's voice somewhere near me, but my vision had tunneled and all I could see was the table and my hands as I laid them flat before me. "Justine, we did it. You did it!"

"Justine! Justine!" My mom ran up to me and flung her arms around me, hauling me up onto my feet. "My baby, oh my God, my baby! You're free!" She kissed my face over and over but I couldn't feel it. My body felt as pliable as putty, like I'd lost control of my muscles, and my temples throbbed willfully, threatening to break my skull apart. But it didn't matter. I didn't care. The night-mare was over.

More faces and noises bounded toward me, and I felt myself being swept away from them, a team of guards helping me and Jack and my parents out of the court-house and into the soft flecks of rain that filled the sky like static, falling one by one onto my arms, my collar-bones, my face, feeling like a million tiny kisses. The falling drizzle lit up with flashbulbs and I didn't even flinch. I held my head high.

Justine, how do you feel? FLASH! Justine, who killed Eva-Kate Kelly? FLASH! Justine, what do you have to say to the folks who doubted you? FLASH! Justine, will you ever forgive your accusers? FLASH! Do you believe the LAPD owe you an apology? FLASH! FLASH! Justine! Justine, over here! FLASH! Can you give us a smile, Justine? FLASH! Justine, do you think you were framed? FLASH! Justine, what do you have to say to everyone who believed in you? FLASH! FLASH! Justine, what comes next? FLASH! FLASII! FLASH! FLASH! FLASH! FLASH! FLASH! FLASH! FLASH!

Being escorted into my mom's Land Rover, I thought again of the day four years ago when I'd had my wis-dom teeth taken out. I'd woken up after what felt like only a moment with the taste of cotton and blood in my mouth, wads of gauze tucked in between my gums and my cheeks. My eyes creaked open to a room that was golden and glowing, an opalescent aura humming off the walls, making a ring around the head of the nurse standing over me. The room and everything in it was so exquisitely beautiful it made my eyes water. There was a joy and an ease and a relief nestled deep in my muscles and in my bones. My blood was a warm, slick stream of rosy silver. I'd found heaven. I'd simply stumbled upon it.

"Angel?" my mom had asked, holding my hand. "How are you feeling?"

I'd surveyed the room once more, blinking, taking it all in. I'd sighed, smiled, and said, "This is the best day of my life."

✳ ✳ ✳

At home I collapsed onto my bed and nuzzled my cheek against the down pillows. My phone rang off the hook— Riley, my dad, Aunt Jillian, Maddie, Abbie, my grandma, dozens of numbers I didn't know. I let it all go to voice mail. On Instagram, the comments flooded in, kind words of praise and congratulations peppered with the occasional malicious epithet.

> **@Christian_Williams:** Congratulations, sweetheart, you deserve only the best!

> **@Michelle1225:** ALL HAIL QUEEN JUSTINE. She walks among us again!

@YourBlueValentine: What an ordeal. I'm so happy it's over. Go enjoy life and don't listen to anyone who tells you otherwise!

@WhatsUpCourtney: 100% innocent and I knew it all along!

@LexiLexi99: You're beautiful and we love you!

@Piper.Precious: Get it, girl.

@TravelGirl04: You're all tripping, this girl is guilty AF. Go home and kill yourself, bitch!

@ToniThaTyger: Congratulations, angel!!! @TravelGirl04 STFU.

@R33LDeal: I'm so happy a bunch of jealous losers didn't take you down!

@GirlieEllie: I <3 this verdict, right?!

@JennieJenny97: You're a killer and you're disgusting. Eva-Kate is gone because of you. Burn in hell, evil whore.

That's enough of that, I thought, tossing my phone aside. I picked Princess Leia up from the floor and let her bite excitedly at my wrists while I felt myself get hypnotized by the rain quietly thrumming against my window. When I closed my eyes I still saw splotches of white camera flash. I wondered if they'd ever go away.

What comes next? a reporter had asked outside the courthouse. The question reverberated now, a tiny pebble rattling through the hallways of my mind. *What comes next? What happens now?*

There was a knock at my door.

"Hello?" I asked, one eyelid popping open.

"It's me," said my mom.

"You can come in," I told her. She opened the door slowly—small groans unfolding from the hinges one by one—and just stood there, hovering. I shut my eyes again and went back to listening to the rain. It was the only sound I wanted to hear for the rest of my life.

"Justine," she said finally, sitting down at the foot of the bed, resting her hand on my ankle. "Listen. A lot has happened, and I know we haven't, you know, had time—or energy, really—to . . . *discuss* everything, but I just wanted to say that I'm going to put the ball in your court, okay? We can talk whenever you're ready, or, if you'd prefer, we don't ever have to talk about it. We can leave it all in the past and move on. Just . . . I know I failed you, and I'm sorry."

I opened my eyes and sat up to face her.

"You didn't fail me," I said. "Your testimony helped *free* me."

"Oh." She seemed taken aback by this, tilting her head like a quizzical puppy. "You're not upset? About . . . ? I just feel that if I were you and—"

"No," I assured her. "I'm not upset."

She sighed deeply.

"That's good to hear, Justine. I'm glad." She squeezed my foot and stood up. "I'll let you rest, but come get me if there's anything you need."

"Actually," I said. "There is one thing."

CHAPTER 23

WHO KILLED EVA-KATE KELLY? THE WORLD WANTS TO KNOW

*I*f I had told my mom that I *was* upset, that I did actually resent her with every fiber of my being, she wouldn't have let me go. And I *had* to go. I had to get out of there, even if just for a few days. I still had some money left from my Hot Toxic sponsorship deal and I used some of the cash to rent myself a room at the Ojai Valley Inn.

My mom had lent me her Land Rover for the trip and I was packing a few things into it, getting ready to go, when I got an unexpected voice mail.

"Hello, Miss Childs, my name is Kenny Kaufman. I'm Eva-Kate Kelly's attorney. If you have the time, I'd like you to come to my office to sign a few things so that you can take possession of what Miss Kelly left to you."

Left to me? I hung up the phone feeling giddy and wide-eyed. *Me? In Eva-Kate Kelly's will?*

After everything. For a glimmer of a moment, I hoped. *Maybe she really did care about me.*

✳ ✳ ✳

The offices of Kaufman & Kaufman were located in Pacific Palisades, right off the PCH, and conveniently on my way to Ojai. I pulled up in the Land Rover listening to "Teardrops on My Guitar (Pop Version)" from Taylor Swift's debut album, blown away and deeply touched by the fact that one person could be so innocent and so brilliant at the same time. God, I wanted to be her. I wanted to be somebody who could get knocked down over and over and over but never stop standing right the fuck back up.

"Miss Childs." Kenny Kaufman smiled as he pulled a leather wingback chair out for me. "Thank you for coming on such short notice. As you're underage, I'd normally have asked for you to have a parent or guardian with you, but Eva-Kate instructed otherwise, at least for this initial conversation." He had a nice face, I thought, symmetrical and safe with white stubble and scholarly black-rimmed glasses. The tip of a green tie rested on his belly, which protruded behind a blue shirt with white pinstripes and collar, the kind of shirt you always saw on men in eighties movies about the stock market.

"Of course." I smiled back, trying hard to curb my curiosity, at least enough so that it wouldn't break out in an inappropriate grin across my face. "So, what's up?"

"What's up," he said, dropping a small stack of papers in front of me, eyes twinkling, "is that Eva-Kate left a will. And she, well, she wanted you to have a few things."

"Okay . . . what did she want me to have?"

"Her car, for one."

"*Her car?* The Audi? Are you sure?"

"I'm sure." He nodded. "And that's just the beginning."

"What do you mean?"

"Well, in addition to her car, it seems she left you her home in Venice, as well as all her financial assets."

"She left me . . . everything?" My insides squirmed. Sometimes extremely good news and extremely bad news can feel exactly the same, like a plunge into nothingness.

"I'm sorry it had to come to you under such unfortunate circumstances, and, of course, if the verdict had gone the other way we wouldn't be having this conversation, but you're now the owner of a periwinkle Audi S7 and the house at Eighteen Carroll Canal. Or you will be once you turn eighteen and reach the legal age of inheritance. Arrangements can be made for a conservator to manage the assets for you until then, and for you to have use of them."

"But wh-why?" I stammered. "I mean, why me? She had so many friends. She had a family."

I should have been happy, excited. I was rich now,

officially, after all. But I was too self-conscious. I felt as though Eva-Kate were watching me then, handing me the keys to her car and home from beyond the grave. Was this another test? Would she be testing me for the rest of my life?

"I don't know," he said, handing me an envelope. "But maybe this will help explain. She left you a note."

I tore open the envelope and dropped it to the floor. The note was written on pink personalized Eva-Kate Kelly stationery with a black ink Micron pen. It read:

To Justine,
If you're reading this, well, I'm dead. You may
be wondering why I've chosen to leave you all
my stuff, and the answer is twofold. 1. You
understand me, the most anyone ever has, and
you see me for who I really am. Or maybe you see
me for who I want to be. (Yikes, I mean, wanted.
Past tense since I'm dead now LMAO.) 2. I love
you. You're the most beautiful person I've ever
known, inside and out, and I only wish we could
have had more time together. In this fake plastic
world, where everything is just an illusion, you
were my reminder of the real.
I hope you'll miss me.

Lots of love,
Eva-Kate

When my heart finally stopped pounding, I arranged to meet with Kenny Kaufman the following week to discuss estate management and conservators and possibly the legal emancipation of a minor. That minor being me. It was too much to think about right now. Then he walked me out to the car.

"Hey, I have one more question," I said, pulling open the door. "When did Eva-Kate write the will?"

"When she bought her house," he said. "In the beginning of June. But she added the note later."

She wrote me into her will before we'd ever met, I thought, and craved her madness. I wanted her madness right there with me, pressed up against me until it blended with my own. The entire time I knew her, I had no knowledge of her obsession. Had she no knowledge of mine? I never thought I'd have to be afraid of her. Did she know she should have been afraid of me?

"Oh," I said. "Just wondering."

"By the way," he said as I slid into the front seat, "congratulations on the verdict. I knew you were innocent all along."

✖ ✖ ✖

Driving north along the water, I passed through Malibu, still scorched and smoky from recent fires. The flames had been extinguished, but the sky still burned, glaring down like a pair of irritated eyes, blood vessels stinging red.

I kept thinking that I should be listening to *Reputation*, Taylor's darkest album, the edgiest album, the only album written after the Old Taylor had died. Just like me, I thought, Taylor had been wrongly accused, and *Reputation* had been her chance at self-defense. But I'd listened to it hundreds of times just this past month and was thirsty for a taste of something new.

After "ME!," which had been released in April, there were three new Taylor Swift songs I'd been too distracted to listen to. It was early August now, and it was time. Of the four songs, I liked "The Archer" and "Lover" best, two impressively vulnerable pleas to love itself. In "Lover," when Taylor sang, "Can I go where you go? Can we always be this close?" a tear slid down my cheek and I thought about that first night with Eva-Kate on her balcony. That first night with the moonlight in her bubble-gum-colored hair, her lips brushing against mine, how I thought it could really be something. And in "The Archer," when Taylor sang, "Who could ever leave me, darling, but who could stay?" I wiped my tears away, thinking about the athame as it entered Eva-Kate, as she fell off the bridge and into the water. Splash.

✳ ✳ ✳

The Ojai Valley Inn lay sprawled out over acres of rolling, velvety emerald green. Spanish Colonial Revival buildings painted white with brown terra-cotta roofs, palm trees and pear trees and sycamores sprouting up among golf courses and crystal-clear pools beneath a sky that was so crisply blue it looked like you could crack it with a spoon.

The Ojai Valley Inn was more spectacular than I'd imagined. And I'd imagined it for quite some time. In 2010, when Benji Laramore left Rachel Ames for Dominique Le Bon, Rachel retreated to the Ojai Valley Inn, where she stayed hidden for ten months, waiting out the paparazzi spree. Her therapist went with her. The therapist called her daughter back in LA once a week to check in. She told her about the massages and the saunas, the cabanas and the champagne cocktails and the celebrities who came and went ineffectively incognito. And her daughter, that eight-year-old, would have done anything for an invitation.

A bellhop named Carl carried my suitcase to room 221 wearing a bashful smile on the elevator ride up, avoiding eye contact to the best of his ability. He let me into my room, unloaded my bags off the gold-plated trolley, and then hovered awkwardly in the doorway for a moment. I panicked, not knowing how much to tip, so I fumbled in my wallet and handed him a fifty-dollar bill.

"Uh . . ." His cheeks blushed crimson red. "Thank you, Miss Childs, you're very kind."

Thank God. I sighed, relieved. The last thing I wanted then was for a bellhop to go around telling people I'm a bad tipper.

"Of course." I smiled. "Have a great one."

"You too." He nodded his head. "And hey," he added on his way out, "congratulations."

❈ ❈ ❈

The room was air-conditioner cool and smelled of mint and lavender. A king-sized bed with puffy, swolle , down-pregnant pillows practically bursting at their se ns lay on top of a royal-blue quatrefoil lattice–patterned arpet that stretched from the front door to the wall-lengt win-dows overlooking a lusciously grassy knoll. Purpl vel-vet armchairs sat perched in front of a built-in firep e. A sculpture—a cluster of silver lily pads—hung ab e the mantel.

What would I do next? With my life, I mean. I wa suddenly a free woman; I had money, notoriety, and rivi-eras, as Lana Del Rey says, so what would I do next?

In *White Noise* by Don DeLillo, the main character, Jack Gladney, teaches Hitler studies. A course he invented himself. At one point in the novel, a colleague says to him, "What you did for Hitler, I want to do for Elvis." Or something like that. I imagined moving to New England and teaching Taylor Swift studies. She deserved that, and maybe I deserved to live that kind of life, peaceful, idyllic, writing my own ticket, literally writing the curriculum of my life.

"I'm a fucking queen," I said, throwing myself onto the bed. The pillows were so sumptuous I wanted to take a bite. My stomach rumbled. I thought of those pathetic little ice cream cups and their pathetic little wooden spoons. I called room service and ordered a hot fudge sundae, then called back and added an old-fashioned to the order.

When it arrived, the sun was setting, toxic pink bleeding out across the horizon. I pulled on the plush hotel robe and slipped my feet into the too-large spa slippers in the closet and took my celebration dinner onto the balcony. I sank my spoon into the vanilla ice cream and, for the first time since it happened, I let myself think about that night. I was finally in the clear, so maybe it was safe. I let myself think about the sun rising outside my mom's office window and how I felt after reading all those notes. How I wanted to talk to Eva-Kate, to hear it from her. To tell her I knew everything and that it was all okay because even though I didn't understand why she'd moved across the canal, or why she'd never told me about being my mom's patient, I could never see her as anything other than perfect. In that moment nothing else mattered. I had this one-of-a-kind, perfect person in my life, and I wasn't going to let her go over a lie.

But Eva-Kate didn't like hearing about the notes, that I'd read through them all, learned her secrets. A violation, she called it. She told me we couldn't be friends anymore, that I should pack up my things and leave. She shouldn't have done that. But more importantly, earlier in the night, I shouldn't have grabbed the athame from where it rested next to the answering machine and stuffed it into my sweater pocket.

You might be confused right about now, but try to understand: I wanted to find out who could have done it, because it couldn't have been me. You understand that, don't you? I had to find an answer that made sense, a murder that made sense. But I failed. There was no version that made sense. There was only one moment, apple-rotten and sour, one Etsy-ordered witchcraft athame, and me.

Melinda Warren and the tabloids were wrong about me. I didn't do it on purpose, and I'm not a sociopath. It's just that sometimes, when it's four in the morning and you haven't slept and reality is wearing so thin it feels like tissue paper breaking apart in your hands, and you're feeling so much more than you ever wanted to feel, things get out of control.

Don't get me wrong, I'm not saying that I killed Eva-Kate Kelly. I'm just saying that if I did, it might have happened like this.

❈ ❈ ❈

We got home from San Luis Obispo that night around nine. I went upstairs and heard the voice mail from my mom. I don't know why the athame was sitting there on the ledge next to the answering machine, but I grabbed it. I was afraid and it was an impulse. When you learn your new best friend has secretly been a patient of your own mother's and didn't tell you, you know something is wrong and want to protect yourself.

Eva-Kate came upstairs and I shoved the athame into my pocket. I didn't see Josie, but I guess she saw me. And she watched as we went downstairs. She didn't see me go home. But I did go home, back to my mom's, where I broke into her file cabinet. I was unnerved and unsettled that the combination code was Eva-Kate's birthday, and at first I was unnerved and unsettled by what I read. But that didn't last long. Soon I was flattered, then I was elated. Eva-Kate was fascinated by *me*. *She* had fixated on *me*. The obsession was truly mutual. And that could only be a good thing, I thought. I thought I had to tell her how I felt, tell her I knew how she felt, so that we could be together, so that we could be the perfect match. We *were* the perfect match. Or were we two totally blank screens primed for projection?

I didn't go to the Ace. Well, not yet. I went back to Eva-Kate's after reading through all my mom's notes and found her sitting alone on the bridge in between our homes.

"You came back!" She jumped up to hug me. "I'm so

happy to see you, you don't even know." Her eyes were dazzled and dazzling and wild, like they'd just been awakened to something. I wondered what she was doing out there by herself, but I didn't ask.

"I'm happy to see you too," I said, still embraced in her silk-soft arms. "I'm happy to be back." We had only been apart for some hours, but it had felt like forever lingering in limbo.

"I've had such a weird night," she said. "I can't begin to tell you. But, listen, I'm sorry that I didn't—"

"It's okay." I took her hands. "I understand."

"You do? Do you forgive me? I really feel horrible that—"

"I'm not mad," I said. "And, look, I probably shouldn't have, but I read through my mom's notes, and I know you've been interested in me for a long time, and you should know I feel the same way about you. I mean, I think you're the most fascinating person alive, the most magical and enigmatic and—"

"Wait." She stepped back, dropping my hands. "You read those notes? Everything from, like, my private sessions with my therapist?"

"With my mom, yeah. But you don't need to be upset. I'm not mad and I don't judge you. If anything it just made me love you more."

"That's really fucked up." Her eyes dropped. "I don't know what to say."

"No, it's not," I said, though I knew she was right. "I shouldn't have read them, but I was scared that you'd lied to me all summer and I just had so many questions. Can you understand that I just wanted some answers?"

"That doesn't give you a reason to disrespect my privacy, Justine." Her eyes went completely cold. "This is a huge violation. Like, huge."

"I didn't . . ." My mind reeled. I shouldn't have told her. Now I'd ruined everything. Again. I always ruined everything. "I didn't mean it that way. Please, just try to see—"

"No." She crossed her arms. "Absolutely not. I need you to leave."

"*Leave?* No, Eva-Kate, listen to me. I'm so sorry I read the notes, but you kept this big secret from me all summer. In a way, aren't we even? We're the same, Eva-Kate, we're two pieces of a whole and we need each other."

"I don't need you," she laughed. "I don't even want you. You really should leave."

"I'm not going to leave. You're scared but I'm not going to let you push me away."

"You're pathetic." She took a step toward me. "You're so desperate to be close to me, to be part of my life, my world, but you never will be, not after what you just did. You can go inside, pack your stuff, and then get out of my way because I literally never want to see your mediocre, nobody face again."

Maybe if the situation had been just a little different, I would have only pushed her, maybe I would have slapped her. But I had the athame in my pocket, and so in that moment of hurt, without thinking, I stabbed her. Her eyes popped. When she realized what had happened, she smiled.

"Damn," she said. "You're fucking crazy."

And then she was gone. It only took seconds, the light and color draining from her face, blood rushing from the wound above her belly. My mind went blank, a completely empty expanse, white hot and buzzing. I checked for a pulse and there was none.

I panicked. I unlocked her phone (061300, a good guess). On the screen when it opened was a text exchange with somebody called Silver Fox. Silver Fox? I tried to think: Who did Eva-Kate know who could be considered a silver fox? I had no idea. I know now that it was Dr. Silver.

I miss you, Princess, Silver Fox had texted.

I miss you too, I texted back, *come over.*

I rolled her body off the bridge and into the water.

Then I went to the Ace.

Like I said, sometimes things just get out of control.

ACKNOWLEDGMENTS

I want to thank the following people for their help, love, ideas, and support as I wrote this book: Scott Antonucci, Richard Abate, Spencer Bly, Birdie Bly, Melissa De La Cruz, Hannah Denyer, Omar Doom, Krista and Kelly Doyle, Quinn Falconer, Kate Farrell, Caroline Kepnes, Natasha Lipson, Jack Lipson, Shiloh Lisbon, Erin Mallory Long, Breann Loveless, B.J. Novak, Ruby Post, Alexis Sanchez, Arpy Sarkissian, Ali Segel, Theresa Smith, Jason Solano, Kellen Solano, Cameron Solano, Scarlett Solano, Robert Wieder, and Jessica Zaleski.

Thank you once again to my parents, Caron Post and Mark Lipson, for encouraging me to follow my dream of writing books, and for not taking it personally that the parents in this one are awful. I love you and am so lucky to have you.

Thank you to my grandmothers, Ellie and Doreen, for believing in me when I don't believe in myself.

Last but not least, this book would not have been possible without my legal consultant and good friend Brad Kaiserman. Thank you for teaching me everything I know about the legal system and helping Justine get a fair trial.